JO MAY

Gods, Mortals and Mutts

From the birth of earth to the here and now

Copyright © 2023 by Jo May

All rights reserved. No part of this publication may be reproduced, stored or transmitted in any form or by any means, electronic, mechanical, photocopying, recording, scanning, or otherwise without written permission from the publisher. It is illegal to copy this book, post it to a website, or distribute it by any other means without permission.

First edition

*This book was professionally typeset on Reedsy.
Find out more at reedsy.com*

To

What's to come

May God give me strength

May Dogs give me companionship

May Humans not interfere too much

        Jo May

Contents

The Creator	1
Earth Summit	7
Upside-down Legs	11
Fauna and Homo Erectus	19
The Bungalow Zone	24
Failed Soufflé	30
Gadgets	36
The Short End of the Stick	41
Divots and Dopes	49
Whirlpool of Benevolence	55
Hot 'n' Cold	60
Complications	65
Good Things	73
The Best Laid Plans	79
Jo	83
Frank	85
The Creator	86
About the Author	89
Also by Jo May	91

The Creator

The universe was born almost fourteen billion ago. It's very existence is thanks to the indefatigable efforts of deity known simply as **The Creator**. *Here (approximately!) is what happened ...*

Back in the misty half-light of the dawn of time, The Creator had a meeting with his number two, an entity called Aidrian. That's Aidrian with an extra 'i', as in Aid. The second 'i' also gave him visual depth perception which was a bonus when working out distances between galaxies - or catching a ball or stabbing a meatball with a fork. Because this was the time before anything at all the meeting should have taken place in the pitch black and in utter silence. But they weren't in the dark because The Creator had made a 60-watt table lamp which illuminated his tiny capsule in the infinite blackness, and conversation was possible because he had also formulated an inert gas through which sound travelled. Clever chap, eh? This meeting consolidated their ideas and the universe was conceived. At zero hour, the Creator and Aidrian donned their crash helmets and ....

BOOM!

A unimaginatively dense particle exploded with great force. The infant universe grew exponentially, expanding at an incredible rate.

'Wow!' said The Creator, as he and Aidrian watched rocks and debris disappear into the distance, in all directions. 'That went well.'

After lunch things settled down a bit and slowly, ever so slowly, gravity drew solar systems together to create fledgling galaxies. This enormous new matrix maintained its shape by huge gravitational forces. Planets were assigned to stars and satellite moons allocated to planets. Swarms of rogue rocks, like plagues of insects, were left to race through space with silent, spinning menace. Achingly slowly, by degrees, things began to cool to the point where rudimentary life began.

'You can turn that light off now,' said Aidrian.

'You're quite right,' replied The Creator. 'Don't want to waste resources.'

Indeed the cosmos was now lit by a billion suns. He and Aidrian knew they had made something special when incredible, multi-coloured nebulae formed, magnificent against the black backdrop of space. With the bang, time's spring had begun to unwind and the universe's multi-billion-year life had begun.

At the beginning, there was only one boss - The Creator. You have to understand that, despite what later accounts claimed, this was the age before religion. Much, much later, the first two-legged beings crawled out of the swamp. Gradually these upright oddities became more secular and argumentative and congregated in larger and larger groups. They were defined by geographical and geopolitical divides and shouted and pointed at one another over improvised borders.

These groups began to dream up their own deities, if for

nothing else so they could eat some festive foods on designated occasions, luxuries such as Christmas Thyme or Ramadan Jam. Early humanoids decided they needed somebody to pray to on a Sunday morning. In addition, they wanted someone to absolve their misdeeds when they'd been on the pillage or stolen a bicycle. Different religions sprung up in different locations. Buddhism, Judaism, Christianity, Islamism, Sikhism and Hinduism, for example, appeared all over the globe. They each worshipped a variation of a supreme being. None matched The Creator in overall majesty, but they nevertheless shone bright in the dark of the cosmos. Most importantly, these man-made deities offered local tribes a sense of spiritual individuality.

As time went on, the tribes squabbled increasingly between each other. Not that they necessarily believed that one religion was better than another – no, it was more about influence, manipulation and cold, hard cash. There was only so much wealth to go around and only so many subjects over whom to rule, so the various groups fought one another in the name of their deity.

Before all that, The Creator and his assistant had to lay the foundations of a potentially civilized world. When things had cooled and settled down a bit, they met to set out their great experiment and chose a planet that would eventually become known as Earth.

'Why that one, Aidrian?'

'Well, it's too big to be destroyed by a rogue meteorite and small enough not to be able to cause too much inter-galactic trouble.'

'Mm, that makes sense. Good one.'

In fact, it was tucked away from anything important in a quiet corner of the universe. It was considered so insignificant, at least initially, that they named the galaxy after a chocolate bar. The planet's name invited much discussion because there was far more water than solid ground. Water, in its fluid form, is rare in the cosmos and Aidrian had rather overdone it while moulding this new world.

'Got a bit overexcited,' he'd explained to The Creator. 'However, it does offer exciting opportunities for evolution because a large proportion of future life will originate from the water. Creatures will need a whole different physiology so it'll be interesting to see what crops up.'

Because of the preponderance of water, they initially thought to call the planet Aqua. After all, its later development called for it to shine a wonderful, vibrant blue in the blackness of space. Aquamarine on black – perfect. However, they realized that Aqua was a bit silly because the final draft of the earthly creatures, Human Beings, or Uprights as they would come to be called, were not scheduled to have gills. Consequently, if they had inhabited the nice shiny blue portion of the planet, Uprightkind would have perished immediately (in evolutionary terms) by drowning. This would likely have brought a premature end to the Great Experiment.

Quite apart from that, The Creator and Aidrian are decent, upstanding beings and did not want to cause undue suffering. At least, not until they could implement one of their later plans and start various savage wars. The plug was pulled on Aqua and they settled on the name Terra.

Then they had second thoughts on that, too. They changed it to 'Earth' because Terra sounded uncomfortably close to the name of The Creator's Uncle 'Terry' who was an unreliable character. In fact, at the time the experiment got under way, Terry was banished to an outpost in the far reaches of the cosmos without a return ticket.

But, wait a minute! You'll notice it incongruous that The Creator should have an elder relative? Surely, as the first of anything, The Creator should be top of the family tree. Ah, yes. But it just shows how much influence the chief deity has over time, space and matter. He created his own uncle. The first recorded miracle. So, finally, the experiment began. Building blocks were in place and the infant planet was left to find its feet.

Much later, about 4.5 billion years in fact, in September 2020 The Creator and Aidrian were joined by Dog Almighty to discuss progress on *"The Great Experiment."*

An explanation is required. Dog Almighty is the Supreme Being of the canines, a noble creature who forced his way into the upper echelons of Earth's management by the simple tenet of being the voice of reason at ground zero. During his time on Earth, he demonstrated more common sense than any Upright, so when his mortal time was up he was invited in. He'd begun as a simple canine but had proved himself invaluable in keeping the Uprights from self-imploding. As a consequence, he was deified. Without doubt, he was one of The Creator's most worthy emissaries and provided his boss with no-nonsense advice.

In fact, not only was he deified, his worth was such that he was elected as the first new board member since the dawn of time. The Creator remains Chairman but Aidrian and Dog Almighty are joint-CEOs. They have much influence and pretty much share the day-to-day running of the project.

One could have expected Aidrian to resent having had his sphere of influence diluted by someone else, but that wasn't the case. He welcomed another executive to share the responsibility; he'd been at it for a long time after all. In a quiet moment he'd admitted to Dog Almighty, *'To be quite honest, Dog, I feel rather buggered. I've been at this for quite a while and welcome an easing of the burden.'*

So, there is a little background. What follows are the official accounts, in a number of instalments, that record meetings between The Creator, Aidrian and Dog Almighty. Interwoven through these official records are a number of 'up-to-the-eon' reports from an Upright called Jo and a canine called Frank who had each written a book called **The Boro** and **Let's be Frank,** respectively. Jo and Frank are acquainted and reside in a scruffy little settlement called Littleborough, floundering in the desolate northern part of Britannia, itself a satellite nation off the coast of Europe.

The audiences took place between September 2020 and January 2023 ...

Earth Summit

1st Board Meeting: 7th September, 2020 – earth calendar

Minutes were taken by Cicero, a former Roman Statesman, because *'he could write a bit.'* (Being a lawyer, Marcus Tullius Cicero had wheedled his way into The Creator's inner sanctum despite a sketchy C.V.)

Dog Almighty and Aidrian approached The Creator, whose name has been abbreviated over the aeons to TC. (*TC also stood for Top Cat, later adopted by a cartoon character on a thing called Television, a plasma box at which the majority of Uprights stare endlessly. The Creator was only addressed as TC by his closest confidantes.*)

'Morning, TC. You got a minute?'
    'Sure, Aidrian, come and sit down. Welcome, Dog. What can I do for you?'
    'It's about our *'Earth'* experiment,' said Aidrian.
    'Aahh.' Pause. 'Yeees.'
    'Quite ... anyway, time for an update. As you remember, we created a suitably sized planet and left it for a while to cool. Way down the line, about 800 million years ago in fact, the environment was suitable for multi-celled organisms to form.

They basically crawled out of a hot swamp and life on earth was underway. From there we allowed evolution take its course. Dog and I have come to report where we're up to.'

'Good, I've been wondering what happened. If memory serves, it was about three billion earth years ago when we launched that project, wasn't it?'

'4.5 to be precise, actually,' corrected Dog.

'Goodness, how time flies.' TC looked off into the distance with a quizzical look on his face, perhaps remembering the early days when his hips were a little less stiff and he didn't have to take a daily Statin.

'Yes, it was quite a time ago,' said Aidrian, 'although we caused some consternation when I went to have a look a couple of thousand years ago.'

TC chuckled. 'Indeed. It took a bit of fancy footwork to get home again.'

'It sure did. Not sure I'd want to go through all that again! I'm not good with enclosed spaces. Or crosses, or treachery. Or those blasted sandals, come to that.' He shivered theatrically. 'What we'd like to do is offer you a moderately optimistic appraisal of where we're up to. To be perfectly frank, there have been a few inconsistencies over the centuries that have made optimism a challenge, but overall we're doing OK.'

'Anyhow, if you remember, that first single cell divided into two. Each half developed a nucleus and slowly, but quite distinctly, two contrasting branches of life developed. The first evolved into flora. There were early lichens, protozoa, ferns, corals, bacteria, and sponges for example. They all lived perfectly happily alongside each other, resolving disputes and adapting to a harmonious existence. In fact, so successful have they been that many thrive today basically unchanged in their original form.

'Indeed,' said TC, 'some of our finest work, I think.' He looked at Dog. 'Well before your time, Dog. You and your kind had the good sense to see how things panned out before making an appearance.'

Dog smiled. 'Aeons, in fact. It's interesting to hear about the early days, though.'

'I agree, Operation Flora has been a triumph,' continued Aidrian. 'However, it's the second branch where things seem to have gone slightly awry. Perhaps you recall the second demi-cell evolved into fauna – in a nutshell animal life. Actually, not a nutshell – that would be flora, but anyway … most species developed and adapted wonderfully well. Some evolved, quite rapidly, into enduring creatures, a few of which continue almost unchanged to this day; millipedes, for example. Others, although thriving for millions of Earth years, were unlucky and were wiped out by cosmic interference.' He looked wistful. 'Perhaps the demise of the dinosaurs was partly our fault but, well, it's too late to worry about that now. Though I think you'll agree they didn't react at all well to that comet. It was a lesson learned.'

'The lesson being,' said Dog with some insight, 'if you want to wipe something out dispatch a large rock.'

'Quite,' replied TC, with a look of regret. 'A drastic intervention, simultaneously unfortunate but effective.'

'What we thought we'd do,' said Aidrian, 'is try and show you something of what goes on at ground level in the present day. Dog and I have decided, for now at least, to focus on a settlement called Littleborough, largely because that is where Dog has his roots. As luck would have it, Dog's half-brother Frank is owned by a creature called Jo, who penned a book about the area. Though I doubt it will reside among literary classics, it was at least an amusing attempt to depict the life within the town. Frank also wrote a book with a dog's eye view of life and they've both agreed to send us an article or two about life in the present on the Blue Planet.'

'Good, I look forward to reading some first-hand accounts of what's going on at the outer reaches of the Milky Way. Right now, though, time for some refreshment I think, so let's pause and reconvene in an hour or so.'

'Here,' said Aidrian, passing TC a folder. 'Here's the first report sent by Frank. Have a read over your cuppa.'

TC thanked his confidante and asked his butler to bring him tea and cake. Aidrian and Dog set off for Apostles Tea Room on the High Street.

(Meeting paused 11.04 AM)

Upside-down Legs

Notes from the Blue Planet by Frank the Terrier.

I've been asked to write a couple of articles that are intellectual, insightful and informative. Sadly, that's not my style, so you'll just have to put up with what you get! Truth be told, I'm glad to be able to contribute because I've heard that Jo (well-known dimwit and my keeper who wrote *The Boro*) has also been asked to write something, and I know full well the kind of drivel he'll be turning out. You guys upstairs deserve a bit of class, so here's the antidote to Jo's written rubble.

I'm not sure how widely these articles will be read, but in case you're unaware I am the dog who wrote *'Let's be Frank'*, fast making a name for itself on the modest-seller list. OK, let's go. To give you a flavour of life on earth, let's just begin with an ordinary day ...

Earth Springtime ...

I'm taking the air with Doug the Pug. We last encountered Doug sporting a flashing headband last Christmas after his owner had dressed him up. Poor Doug was mortified but it all ended well as he managed to sell it to an unsuspecting visitor who happened to be passing through the shire. Today we see him as he should be, 'au naturelle.' We're ambling across a former football pitch, which is now an exercise area that nobody uses. We pause by a *'No Camping'* sign. The sign is working because there's nobody camping. In fact, there's nobody exercising either. I discuss the matter with Doug and we decide we have no ambition to pitch a tent, so we sit down for a breather. Doug's mum and my dad are close by talking about the weather – which doesn't sound very interesting. In fact, I'm writing about somebody talking about the weather, which must be doubly uninspiring – so apologies!

In the middle-distance a horse and rider thunder past a 'No Horses' sign and in the far distance the sun shines brightly on distant moorland.

'How wonderful!' says Doug with a sigh. 'What, with no football, no exercise and no camping, this truly is a little slice of England dedicated to the absence of effort.'

I chuckle. 'Of course, you'd know all about lack of physical endeavour. You will be known by future generations as Douglas the Dilatory.'

'Huh. Very amusing.'

It is early May, the sun is bright and the grass is lush and warm.

Doug says reflectively, 'It's rather clever of The Creator to marry up such gorgeous weather with the Spring daffodils. Imagine sitting in the snow – it wouldn't be half as pleasurable.'

I'm never quite sure whether Doug is being imaginative or dumb, so I sometimes exercise discretion and simply don't respond. But he's right in one respect – the daffodils *are* wonderful. At least those that haven't been mercilessly snapped off or dug up by the Uprights. They take them home and stick them in a pot and stare at them. Then they talk about how nice they used to look outside and bemoan the fact that people no longer respect the environment in which they live. The daffodils that remain unmolested are majestic in bloom and a few bees flit between them gathering dust. It's actually the later varieties of daffodils that are on show; the early ones have already bloomed and are now retreating back into their bulbs ready for a long nap before next year.

This is a good time of year for dogs. Spring, the Uprights have called it. We know we are entering the time of plenty and tails wag with a little more fervour. We realize that with the arrival of the fairer weather, Uprights start to promenade and throw food about. Why they chuck stuff on the floor is a mystery but our larder in the park and on the playing fields is replenished. Like bears emerging from hibernation, we canine vacuum cleaners rev into life and prepare to blitz the great greensward.

'Did I ever tell you the saga of Dad's upside-down legs?' I ask Doug, rather out of the blue. He's dozing, so looks a bit nonplussed by my question.

'No, can't say I remember that one.'

'Poor chap has this complaint where he doesn't get enough blood to his legs. He found out a few years ago he's got some sort of blockage and since then has exercised like a maniac. Far too much for a man his age in my opinion, but what makes it worse is that he usually drags me around with him. I stay pretty fit on the back of his daily routine but I don't half get knackered. I'm referring to his walking here, of course; he does a fair bit of cycling too. Have to admit, I'm not great on a bike. I'm not bad on a skateboard, but the bicycle is somehow not suited to our physical configuration.'

Doug has a roll on his back before laying on his side to get his breath back. A dog of modest fitness is Doug. A companionable silence ensued, broken by the pug, who has obviously been thinking. 'There are a number of Upright activities that don't suit us,' he says reflectively. 'Triple jump is one.'

I judge this one of those moments to keep quiet.

'You tried that?' he asks. I shake my head. 'Last time I had a go, when the Olympics were on, it tuned into a right shambles. Too many moving parts, that's the problem. Ended up with my snout in the mud. I don't think pugs are really the right shape for anything requiring genuine athleticism.'

'Ha! With the greatest respect, lithe you are not. But have you noticed whenever something comes on TV the Uprights reckon they're world-beaters. Tennis and snooker, for example. My Dad is dreadful at both – according to his brother anyway. For tennis he's too short, too slow and too inflexible and snooker is a near impossibility because his eyes are buggered. Quite apart from his general physical deterioration, he's red/green colour blind.'

'You're making it up.'

I chuckle. 'I'm not.'

I continue, 'There was an interesting debate about evolution more than a millennium ago. The gist was that evolution follows its own natural course – which is slow, ponderous and inevitable, like lava from a volcano. Or Dad on his bicycle. It would have been easy for The Creator to interfere and make everything uniform and compatible. Dad could have played tennis with his brother and not been humiliated, and I could have been developed to run as fast as Willy the Whippet. Willy and I could have stood on the top step of the rostrum side by side to collect joint gold medals! Actually, creating everyone equal would mean everybody in the race would be crammed on the top step, so that doesn't make much sense, does it? In fact, had equality been the norm there would be no races - there's no point. Instead, the only competition would be who could LOSE a race. A competition who could come last. That would also be a bit daft because nobody would leave the start line! No, the variety of natural evolution is the answer. The powers that be certainly got that right.'

'We need variety in most areas,' stated Angus the Unruly (soothsayer) in Earth year 974. *'However, the colour-blind issue is debatable. How on earth will Uprights be supposed to wire up a plug if they can't distinguish different colours? Should they ever invent electricity, that is.'*

Doug and I pause as we digest the conundrum of evolutionary law. I think Doug is rather overwhelmed by the debate because he does what Uprights tend to do when they can't answer a question or are too dim to join an intellectual argument - he skirts around the issue. 'You're right,' he says, returning to an earlier point in the discussion where he felt on more solid ground. 'The Uprights blow with the breeze of whichever activity is on telly. My Dad doesn't half grumble when cooking programmes are on because Mum tries all sorts of unlikely combinations. *"What the hell is this supposed to be?"* is a regular refrain when we've had the telly on and she's 'tried a little experiment.' He's a creature of habit is my old man. Happy with his burger and chips. *'Please, no more of this newfangled cobblers'* is one of his familiar requests.' He pauses, then continues on his safe conversational path.

'Running is just about OK for us dogs, but other stuff, not so much. Javelin is a tough one, same with discus. Lack of opposable thumbs is the problem there.'

'And pole vault.'

'Aye, pole vault's another non-starter.'

'And cricket.'

'We should stick to running.'

'Or jogging.'

'Yes. Jogging is more dignified.'

Tramping through the long grass about thirty yards away is the newly crowned hero on the block.

'There he is,' says Doug. 'Our new superstar.'

Acknowledging our gaze, Willy the Whippet gives us a regal nod of the head. Willy has developed into an entrepreneur, a beast who has emerged as a true visionary. He had a dream and followed it through with dogged determination. Most importantly, he had the 'mother wit' to make it a success. He hit on a brilliant idea and combined two of the world's most cherished passions - fast food and ice cream - and ... Mr Whippet was born!

Willy is becoming a legend. He's currently developing a dog-friendly chocolate range to be called Walnut Whippy. Sam the Basset, resident humourist and wit, arrives and sits down. We all enjoy Sam's witty asides and, unfairly perhaps, expect them.

'Hello, Sam,' I say. 'We're just talking about Willy.'

'Aye, he's done well, hasn't he?' says Sam without a trace of either humour or wit, defying my build-up. Then, with more Sam-like conviviality: 'He's done well not to put weight on. In fact, he'll have to maintain his physique or be forced to change his company name to Mr Hefty, which doesn't quite have the same appeal.'

'Shankly (Liverpool-supporting Scouser) is jealous of Willy's fame, I think,' says Doug. 'He's used to being top dog. With more than a hint of scouse malice, Shankly called Willy a 'Fat

Cat' the other day. It was supposed to be offensive, comparing a sleek speedster like Willy to a porky pussy, but Willy just laughed it off. Left Shankly floundering in his wake, if you will.'

Sam continues, 'I don't think Shankly is too keen on Willy being benevolent either. Did you hear he helped Bernard the other day?'

'You mean St Bernard, the one who transcribed our Bible?'

'Aye, the same. I'm sure you're aware that despite being a notable scribe, Bernard is not the tidiest creature. His facial hair, to put it kindly, is rather unruly. Now Willy notices such things and could stand by no longer before asking Bernard if he had an issue with his whiskers. He admitted that his eyesight wasn't all it might be, so trimming his beard was rather a hit-and-miss affair. On hearing this, without a second's thought, Willy dashed home to procure a spare pair of spectacles, which he gave to Bernard.

'There,' he said. 'These should help. Specshavers.'

Sam paused.

'For quips like that he's become known as Witty Willy Whippet.'

'Are you making this up?'

'Of course I am. But I told Shankly the story and he stormed off in a huff. He believed it. Or wanted to. Bernard had actually been to the dog-grooming place up the hill.'

'He does look better, I have to say.'

We fall into a companionable silence and I have momentarily nodded off when awoken by Doug. 'Didn't you start this ramble with something about your Dad's legs?'

'Oh yes. Forgot. Upside-down legs. As I say, he does loads of walking and biking. I'm not sure whether normal people have the same reaction, but all his exercise has slimmed down his thighs and piled muscle on his calves. As a result his legs look upside-down. The thick bit is at the bottom. They're an extraordinary shape, like a couple of misshapen sacks on the back of his legs. It's like he's stocked up on sprouts and stored them down the back of his stockings.'

The manic day wears on ...

Fauna and Homo Erectus

B*oard Meeting recommences.   7th September 2020. Midday.*

'I rather enjoyed Frank's contribution. Will there be another?' asked TC.

'Yes, there's one due any day now. I'll pass it on. There's one just in from the Upright, Jo. It's currently with the translators because it arrived rather muddled. Whether it got mangled on its travels or it was the product of a mixed-up intellect I'm not sure. An intelligible version will be available imminently.'

'Good, I look forward to them both. Thank you.'

'OK, lets move on, said Aidrian. 'So, regarding the evolution of both fauna and animal life, all was progressing pretty smoothly till a couple of million years ago when something called Homo Erectus appeared. They were an illogical and peculiar development and we weren't sure whether The Prince *(referring to The Prince of Darkness, the Devil himself)* had a hand in messing about with some unwilling creature's DNA. However, despite being irregular creatures, particularly in the early days, the Uprights were happy enough. They developed opposable thumbs, mentioned by Frank in his missive, particularly important when playing darts and spanning an octave on the piano.

Simultaneously they developed a higher intelligence than many other strains of fauna and soon realized that they could take over. They decided they needed to dominate, rule over the other creatures, even the weak of their own kind. Rather tyrannical, actually, don't you think?'

'I do detest confrontation,' said TC. 'It just seems all so … unnecessary. Mind you, your water-into-wine trick seemed to be the catalyst for plenty of aggressive behaviour. Ongoing, I might add. These humans seem to have a problem managing the effects of most elixirs. I heard they tried to hide their lack of capacity by changing the original name of 'Murder a Lot' to 'Merlot,' but it fails to disguise their underlying frailties.'

'Yes, unfortunate, but despite that little, uh … wrinkle, at the end of the day we basically let them get on with their own evolution. Frank recognizes this, which is why he is so forgiving of the Uprights' frailties. He seems to understand that they are just going through growing pains and will probably develop some common sense in due course. Besides, we can't afford to intervene too much – it would compromise the data. I'd hate to come to the wrong conclusions. The thought of passing on various creatures' idiocy to future worlds doesn't bear thinking about.'

'I suppose you're right.' TC sighed theatrically. 'Do go on.'

'I can see your misgivings, TC, but ultimately you are The Creator and, as such, not really responsible for the development of each strand of life. There has to come a time when we leave them to get on with their own evolution, however scatterbrained it may appear.'

'I suppose you're right.'

'Right, well Dog and I have spoken at length about this and in our analysis so far. If there is a problem, it revolves around a group who call themselves human beings. The name itself suggests a life-form in some confusion. I've asked around and quite why the word '*beings*' is tacked on the end nobody is sure. 'Humans' on its own would do perfectly well. In due course, humans themselves split in two groups and became known as humans and huwomans. Intrinsically they are the same beast with a few minor physical discrepancies. They subsequently appear to have dropped the title huwoman. But inexplicably and illogically, they lumped everything under the less intelligent brand - 'hum<u>an.</u>' To bring things right up to the present, they are having a ludicrous inter-Upright confrontation about pronouns, for goodness' sake. If one very small section of the population gets their way, 'human' will have to be changed to 'huthem.' Huthem Beings, I ask you!

'Whichever way this latest confusion is resolved, the point is that this branch of evolution seems to have started off as one half of a single cell, progressed quite nicely for a while, then started a major reverse. A direction in which it is still heading. Humans have evolved into something quite unpredictable, to the point of erratic, even reckless at times.'

'Oh dear,' said TC, raising his impressive white eyebrows.

'Quite,' said Dog. 'Not only do they seem hell-bent on destroying all the flora, which is frankly the most attractive evolutionary half, but they also appear to have begun to self-destruct. I don't know if you remember, but when the Uprights created a thing they called the atomic bomb in Earth year 1945, Aidrian sent a memo to the disciples warning that it may be the beginning of the end of 'Experiment Earth.' The Uprights, they warned, had found a way to destroy themselves. And, I might add, everything else as well. They appear to have come quite close to an apocalypse on a number of occasions but pulled back at the last moment. However, the threat remains with the promise of ever-more powerful devices. The whole situation is exacerbated because they insist on choosing leaders of doubtful countenance. There are a few current incumbents who simply wouldn't have the sensitivity to survive if they lived among the sponges.'

Dog sat back and crossed both sets of legs, apparently pleased with his summation of events hitherto.

'Oh Lord,' said The Creator.

'One of the problems,' continued Aidrian, 'was a simple piece of miscommunication. During their early development I sent an emissary to suggest the humans divided earth into regions. I thought it would not only spice up our experiment but also make it more straightforward for the Uprights to govern themselves in more manageable groups.

'Unfortunately, somewhere along the way, 'region' was misspelled as 'religion.' Somehow 'li' got added. Li actually denotes the number fifty-one in one of their ancient languages, which was uncomfortably close to area fifty-two, where our emissary actually landed on earth. So, what they should have had was a number of individually autonomous, peaceful areas. They ended up with eight or nine main 'religions.'

'The spiritual leaders of these other religions are noble deities like yourself, only a level below. They are all utterly trustworthy and, individually, beings of peace and love. The problem is that each religion has a great many followers and within their number exist enough lunatics intent on causing trouble, which they do in the name of their chosen religion. Sadly, this drags down the venerability of the whole shooting-match. Unintended pun there, but you get my meaning. Consequently, the humans, rather than living in harmony, have bickered and battled for aeons. The only useful service that these hostilities perform is to periodically check rampant overnumbering. Of course, that's not too big a deal because we merely withhold a virulent pandemic or two and let numbers recover. The point is that it appears that these so-called 'intelligent humans' cannot be left to their own devices indefinitely.

'Particularly when those devices are explosive in nature,' added Dog.

'Quite,' agreed Aidrian. 'Not only have they developed unnerving, murderous tendencies, they are also failing to develop in positive areas. For example, they have only managed to visit another celestial body on half a dozen occasions, and each of those to their nearest neighbour. Not a great record, I think you'll agree, for a species that considers itself perceptive and resourceful.

'And when they got there they achieve little. They plonked a flag on the moon's surface as claim of territory and walked around a bit, but nothing meaningful for sure.'

'One bloke played golf,' said Dog.

'He had a worse swing than me,' replied Aidrian. 'Thinking about it, that's probably why they put the flag up.'

They broke for lunch here after which TC had a nap, Dog went for a constitutional and Aidrian, now with golf on his mind, went to the driving range to see if he could reproduce the miracle of a straight three-iron.

© Marcus Cicero 2020

The Bungalow Zone

Notes from the Blue Planet by Jo May

Thank you. I am honoured to be asked to submit a couple of reports. If you've read **The Boro**, you'll know that we (that's my wife and I) returned to Littleborough after an absence of nearly 30 years. If, by chance, you have <u>**not**</u> read **The Boro** you will also know that we returned to Littleborough - because I've just told you in the sentence above. Such insight will be a theme throughout! It may get even better.

Initially, we struggled with the changes we encountered, but came to realize that we couldn't turn the clock back. Things would never be the same and we gradually came to accept our new environment. Now, a few years on, we have built a homely shelter out of the rubble of our crumbled past; homely shelter being a reference to both bricks and mortar and the town to which we have returned. Both are warm, both safe.

Were my previous musings rather downbeat? No, they were straight-talking. Besides, reading is a subjective matter, and everyone interprets a story in their own way. From my point of view, they were honest musings. Thing is, what we found is not of our making, it is our interpretation of what has changed. No blame, I think – nobody made the place busier on purpose; it's obvious it has just evolved, brick by brick, pothole by pothole. Of course if you stay in a particular place full-time the changes are gradual, so you barely notice. It's like not seeing a child for a few weeks – you notice change. But if you live with them day after day, you don't really notice. We came back and certainly noticed that the place had changed. It had evolved, or perhaps devolved. Our choices? Stay or go. Of course, we've stayed; there's still plenty of good things – the people mainly.

The house we have chosen is a bungalow, one of a couple of dozen on a 'development.' Bungalows are traditionally for older folk who have a preference for everything being on one level – no uphill stretches in other words. A collection of single-story dwellings is known colloquially as the waiting room to the world beyond. A place where people sleep late and spend most days not achieving much.

BUT, we oldies are a positive lot. We have to be, frankly, because time may be short and we want to look upon things as 'glass half-full.' In fact, Deidre recently pointed out that if you're glass is half empty, you should simply fill it up. Preferably with a decent quality red wine. We chuckled at that. A simple life-enhancing philosophy that both cheers you up and anaesthetises you against angst. For example, should your neighbour's cat happen to tinkle on your petunias and you want to avoid an unpleasant confrontation, don't rush round and slug your neighbour in the temple, instead top up the wine glass and doze off in front of Gardeners' World.

We (the oldies) had a meeting recently (it's nice to get together to reassure ourselves that we've all survived the weekend) and decided if there is one thing we would like to change about getting older, it's that our bodies should stay in slightly better condition for longer. We don't mind getting older, per se; we're just not keen on getting increasingly pathetic. As one optimist put it, *"I'm happy to be older – I am no longer constrained by my awkward, younger self."* So, Mr Creator (if you're listening) there's probably not much you can do at this stage but if you're starting again with another civilization it may be a point worth considering.

To emphasize, some of the most basic tasks can become a challenge. Something as simple as picking an item up off the floor, for example. To start with, it's a long way down and our actions are dependent on which specific ailment is most uncomfortable on any given day. We have to choose which bending-over method we employ. What's the most nagging ache today? Back, hip, shoulder, knees – the technique is different in each case. Whichever, it's best to have something to lean on for the return journey, like a sturdy coffee table or a chair with which you can heave yourself upright. There's little worse than being sprawled out on the carpet waiting for the emergency services.

Top tip: it's worth putting the TV on before you begin the bending procedure so, if you do get stuck, you have some company. The downside of this is that you might get stuck with some utter drivel. Actually, thinking about it, that could be worse than the indignity of being marooned. Forget the TV idea!

The very act of bending can result in any number of involuntary noises. Creaks, groans, expulsions – they're all possible and we've all become used to expecting the unexpected. *'Senior tumult'* my younger brother calls it – *'prompting involuntary escapes.'* The answer to all this? Leave the object for someone else to pick up, someone younger and more nimble. Or don't drop it in the first place.

Yes, we residents of the bungalow zone are a right old mixture. Some of us can barely walk, particularly frustrating as we wait for distant surgical procedures. Some of us are a touch hard of hearing; for others, balance is not what it was. Try putting a sock on with your eyes closed; it's nigh on impossible without falling over sideways. This eyes closed/balance deterioration is unavoidable; it just happens as we age.

There is a scorched-earth pathway between our neighbourhood and the pharmacy. Perhaps they should consider opening a satellite office on the avenue, or at the very least provide a mobile service like the old travelling libraries. Remember them, when you could pick up a copy of the Adventures of Tintin without it having been redacted? Being a (modest) writer, I have some affinity with Tintin because he is described as *'a multi-talented reporter.'* Much the same as me – if you remove one word!

Priorities change. I used to have the stockbroker on speed-dial – these days it's the dentist. Actually, that's not true – annoyingly it's their answering service I get, not a person. Very professional having someone, or something, deal with your inquiries. Very Harley Street. But, and a big but, this is not Harley Street; this is the A58 in the north of England, where we expect no-nonsense dealings with no-nonsense receptionists with no-nonsense hair-dos and a big smile! Besides, it's good to chat.

Incidentally, the chap who used to look after my modest cash reserves had a catchy slogan: *'Guaranteed to erase all your money worries.'* Which he subsequently amended after a bad year by removing the last word!

In the senior world, days are broken into sessions. Get up, have breakfast and begin session one – aka, the morning. Lunch, then session two. Dinner and session three. The evening session is when we wind down after the fever of sessions one and two. Session three might involve nodding off in an electric chair - the type that helps you to your feet when you awake desperate for the lavatory, as opposed to one that might kill you like 'Old Sparky' - with a bit of luck.

Liberally scattered among the meals and sessions is a mountain of medication. Wasn't there a religious figure, mentioned in a text (religious text, that is, not the 4G telephone sort), who set off into the desert in search of tablets? He probably started mankind's infatuation with medication.

Ultimately, it's wise for the decrepit among us to preload the anti-inflammatories before physical exertion. Then have a beta-blocker afterward to calm a racing heart. Later, we'll likely need something to help with the wicked acid reflux of a prawn madras - a spicy number that never used to bother us. Then a sleeping pill. After two hours tossing and turning, three visits to the lavatory and having to let the dog out in the middle of it all, it's time for our 75 mg Aspirin, breakfast and session one again ... life is a whirl.

Jobs that used to be accomplished in a few minutes (for example, that precious half hour between coming home from work and the evening meal) now take a full morning. Mowing the lawn, for example. A simple, straightforward undertaking you would have thought, but somehow we manage to pad the time out to fill a 'session.' Untangle the chord, clean all the crud off from last time, chat to a neighbour over the fence; all these things take valuable time. We somehow add a zero to the time taken. Twenty minutes becomes two hundred. Three and a half hours to do a piddling little job. *'Buggering about,'* my brother calls it! '*It's living the dream*,' I tell him. The retirement dream of idling the time away and achieving nought if we feel like it -

which seems frequently.

We've learned not to open a conversation with, 'How are you?' That's very dangerous. It's a polite, simple greeting, yet there's a danger that it will be taken at face value and a detailed answer might take us deep into next week. We like to sympathize with one another, but we have to acknowledge the practicalities of life - time is not infinite and there's likely a lawn to mow or a patio to de-weed.

Failed Soufflé

B*oard meeting. June 23rd, 2021 - Earth calendar*

(TC, Dog and Aidrian had finished their previous meeting in time for lunch last September. Unfortunately, time sort of ran away with them. Aidrian had been practising his golf while TC had nodded off - for six months. Dog waited patiently in the shade of a lime tree reading an Agatha Christie mystery and eating Jelly Babies. Time is unimportant in the vastness of the cosmos.)

'OK, where did we get to last time?' asked Aidrian.

'The moon had just escaped a conquering,' said Dog.

'Oh yes. The other-world, cosmic adventures of the Uprights undertaken with timidity and a paucity of success. However, it leads sweetly on to our hypotheses as to why things are deteriorating so alarmingly.'

Aidrian suddenly clammed up and looked out of the window, apparently lost in thought. Dog looked on, willing Aidrian to burst back into life. TC just sat and waited patiently while his assistant obviously battled his demons. TC was sympathetic because he could well understand the pressure of developing a civilization. In actual fact, the reason for Aidrian's mental disappearance was because he couldn't shake the horrors of his golf practice. His final shot had fired off, inexplicably, at right angles, felling a horse in an adjacent meadow. Thankfully the beast recovered, but when asked by his friend Peter Apostlethwaite how his practice had gone, Aidrian had replied simply, 'Mare!'

The Creator coughed politely to return his assistant from wherever his mind had ventured.

'Oh, sorry. Yes. I was about to tell you of the Uprights' nemesis. It transpires they have invented something that has changed things beyond all recognition, called the Internet. Basically, it's a conduit along which bad news and non-intellectual garbage can circulate the globe at the speed of light. Our observers tell me, for I have neither the capacity nor will to understand the concept, that it has the potential to do some good. Unfortunately, it appears to have taken on a persona of its own. It's not easy to figure out who's in charge but from what we can see it appears to be presided over by something called DG, based in a cave in Scarborough. To make matters worse Scarborough is a settlement which unfortunately finds itself in the gloomy territory of Yorkshire.

'DG? I shall explain to the best of my ability. Initially there were two acronyms: DG and GOD. We believe they stood for Drivel Generator and Generator of Drivel, respectively. Frankly, even the most insensitive creature could interpret GOD as derogatory, even insulting. Imagine how the religious feuds could have escalated had they kept that name. Consequently, we believe that DG emerged as the favoured title. It didn't happen without discussion because DG also represents Director General. The problem with that is that by the time an Upright became old and wise enough to become a Director General, they were deemed too important to make day-to-day decisions. So, in effect, a Director General didn't direct at all, they just sat in a large car drinking Pimms. Thus, DG came to represent Drivel Generator, which seems to encapsulate all the Internet is about.

'DG appears to have the ability to manipulate and alter human minds.

Whenever anybody enters the Internet room, their personality changes. Not only that, they also lose whatever common sense they may have had when they arrived. It seems that Uprights send meaningless words and phrases on an uncharted course to be received by anyone who's front gate happens to be open at that particular moment.

'As far as we can see, the collective noun for this huge mass of words is 'gibberish.' This was subsequently changed to 'drivel' because nobody could agree on whether gibberish was two 'b' or not two 'b.' They have been practising the art of drivel for over a half a century through television, but it has really come to maturity with 'DG's Folly.'

'Presumably there is a drivel depository somewhere from which anyone can pluck an absurd, often unsuitable, word or phrase. Humans stare blankly into this 'manufactured matrix of mayhem' (aka the Internet) through what we believe to be plasma-boxes. They delve into this mystical library of drivel, gather words, assemble them in random order and fire them off into the unknown. The only precondition of these messages is that they must be utterly meaningless. Should anything logical actually appear, so endangering the integrity of the drivel, it is immediately dispatched by something called a moderator, who we think is one of a group of umpires carefully monitored and operated by DG. We have discussed this at length and one theory is that a large proportion of Uprights are trying to attain the same level of intellect as a sponge. With success in some quarters, it has to be said.'

Aidrian and Dog chuckled to one another while TC looked at them with raised eyebrows, eyes wide in alarm.

'Sorry to laugh,' said Aidrian, 'but I find it hard to believe that the Uprights can make such a hash of something which is potentially so life-enhancing. The fault lies with administration, I think for two reasons. Firstly, those who oversee the whole shooting match are only in place because they own the hardware or matrix, or whatever it is. In other words, without them, there wouldn't be an Internet. Secondly, the foot-soldiers they've employed to monitor content are so dim-witted that nobody can possibly follow their logic. This means that mountains of trivia and pointless nonsense is shot round the world like an uncontrolled vortex of tripe.

Dog interjected, 'I'm afraid that unless things change, it can only get worse. We, the canine branch, have devised our own system called the World Wide Wag. It is closely monitored by our brightest minds so we can restrict it to premium content only. Hah! If only our food was chosen with as much care. For example, on the Wag if you need something specific you paw in your request and are offered a carefully targeted selection of options. With a click or two of your keyboard you have available the object of your desire. The Upright version is so complicated and convoluted that people have been known to sit at their plasma screens to look for something specific and not re-emerge for many days. They re-join the real world with a manic, thousand-yard stare and need a long walk with their canine companion to regain a modicum of equilibrium.'

'Succinctly put, Dog,' said Aidrian. 'It's a pity really because the vocabulary developed by the Uprights over the centuries, in different languages too, could be used for works of beauty and interest. In fact, in small, isolated pockets, it still is. Sadly, it's largely been hijacked by the majority Cretin tribe. Nobody seems to know the origin of the Cretins, save to say that, thanks to the Internet, their stock has spread at lightning speed and they now inhabit every corner of Planet Earth, rather like Salt & Vinegar crisps - whatever they are. The Cretins have developed into a powerful, if dim, body. I say 'developed' in the context of something moving on, but 'regressed' may be more accurate.

'And, TC, it gets worse,' said Dog mournfully. 'Not only is the Internet mentally divisive, but it's also not much good for physical well-being either. We have numerous reports of humans sitting before their plasma lightboxes for days, even months, on end. Their deportment is something similar to that witnessed after particularly intense battles during the religious conflicts. Humans stare into the middle distance and mumble, as if their spirit is gone and they have lost the will to live, rather like the humans we witnessed from Lancashire.'

'Furthermore, because they sit upright for lengthy periods, any loose flesh - pectorals and bosoms, for example, drift south. It all ends up in a soggy mess around the lower torso/hip area. Rather like a failed soufflé. One of our researchers described these plasma-box devotees as, and I quote, "*flabby digital flies trapped in a specious, synthetic web suspended in a counterfeit world.*" I gave Rasheed the morning off for that effort.'

'Another downside to this Internet phenomenon is happening as we speak,' said Aidrian. 'Remember we sent them a pandemic a while back?'

'Oh goodness. Let's just hold it there for now if you don't mind. I've heard whispers about this and feel I may need to fortify my constitution before we continue. Can we hold it till tomorrow?'

'By all means,' said Aidrian as Dog nodded agreement.

Meeting suspended 11.45 AM

© Marcus Cicero 2021

Gadgets

More notes from the Blue Planet by Jo May

This piece, Mr Creator, is indicative of how we Uprights have replaced natural apparatus (like clubs) with modern alternatives (Rocket Propelled Grenades). An extreme example, I admit. In general, though, we become increasingly reliant on gadgets and implements. Take weeding (or de-weeding); none of this bending down nonsense these days - no, from the Garden Centre we procure a long wooden stick with a blade on the end. A simple, basic tool that allows us to remain approximately vertical while weeding. Somehow *'a stick with a sharp bit on the end'* manifests as thirty-odd pounds at the checkout. *'I'm on a pension, you know'!*

Maybe it's expensive because it's made of bamboo, the price of which has rocketed. Nowadays at the bamboo market there's intense competition between the gardening implement conglomerate and the Giant Panda keepers looking for sustenance for their charges. Whatever they're made of, the quality isn't great and they never seem to last long before we invariably end up with a bent chopper.

Incidentally, bamboo is an example of a fad to which we Uprights seem to take on a whim. It's not the easiest thing to follow but, because a small minority are suddenly worried about too much of a particular gas in their atmosphere, they have started putting bamboo to all kinds of peculiar uses. It's not only the preferred material for garden chopper handles, it's now, astonishingly, used in the manufacture of toilet paper and underwear. You would think that undergarments made from sticks would be most uncomfortable, but it seems that risking a twig up your back passage is favoured over an excess of atmospheric gas. The latest news is that Giant Pandas are on the verge of extinction because too many of us are wearing their food source around our private parts.

Another weed-removal option is a flame-thrower, but you need good insurance and a strong constitution to blaze away with one of those, particularly if you've got a wooden fence. Poison is also an alternative, the ultimate solution one might say, but be careful if next door's cat is a regular visitor. But for sure, the days are gone when we get down on hands and knees and hack away with an old butter knife. Getting down is OK, but you have to be near a sturdy trellis to scramble back up again. And there's no TV to keep you company in the garden should you happen to end up prostrate on the patio.

Right, Mr Creator, I hope I've painted a realistic picture of a few of our elderly adversities. Not that I request or expect a response; it's just good to offload sometimes and, as I say, it may give you an idea or two for your next creations. Thank you for listening.

Actually, on reflection, there is one huge plus to getting on in years. I'm not alone that I enjoy sharing the neighbourhood with people of similar age. Almost without exception we are all polite, respectful and ready for a friendly chat or a laugh. We love to exchange pleasantries and chuckle at one another's difficulties. There's always something to brighten a day.

Last week, for example, I gave my neighbour a laugh when I told him about taking my car through the car wash. I was waved in by the attendant till my front wheel engaged with the travelator, the constantly moving belt that pulls cars through the 'fully automated' car wash. All looked to be progressing as expected – the brushes and equipment started to pass my window and I relaxed into an anticipated three minutes of whooshing and whirring. Then there was a loud knocking on the rear of the car. Rather than being pulled through, I had inadvertently put the car into reverse gear instead of neutral and I was reversing out! I was heading towards the car waiting behind and in danger of flattening the alarmed attendant. I was fortunate to avoid mechanical or personal calamity. Luckily, I still have the reactions of a striking cobra so was able to bring my backwards progress to a speedy halt. It's nice when things go a bit wrong – we have something to chuckle about. If everything went smoothly life wouldn't be half as interesting.

I knew very well what the people in the car wash queue would be thinking! *'Dozy old duffer!'*

We tend to slow down as we age. My old golfing pal was getting pretty ancient, probably just starting his tenth decade, but was still driving his car – albeit slowly. We always joked that if there was a traffic jam in the town, it was either temporary traffic lights or my mate holding everybody up.

It's catching up with me now, too. Are you taking note, Mr Creator? I think you'll find that my difficulties, caused by the ageing process, are not uncommon. The problem is that our minds hurtle along in top gear while our bodies dawdle along behind in second. Witness this passage that contains an age-related little exchange ...

The Olympic motto, eminently achievable in our youth, is now but a distant memory. 'Higher Faster Stronger' has been cruelly doctored to become 'Lower Slower Feebler.' Many seniors need an 'intervention' after a couple of laps with the lightweight electric lawn mower. An artificial stimulant like an energy drink is required - or a nap. Or both. Plus a call, perhaps, to the lad who does the garden across the road. He's ever so quick. And neat. And young. And he can bend down to pick up his rake without ingesting half a pound of anti-inflammatory tablets. Damn him!

I bought an E-bike to try and keep up. Not with the Tour de France lot, more those who amble along in their eighties.

I passed a chap leaning on a wall the other day. He was watching the world go by while eating a sandwich. He was younger than me by some margin. As is my wont, I decided to stop for a chat.

'You look to be struggling on that bike,' he said, as I drifted to a stop. 'You could do with an electric one.'

'It is electric.'

'Oh. Right.' He laughed. 'You forgotten to plug it in then?'

I was dawdling, I admit. But why couldn't he say something nice instead of ripping my self-esteem to shreds? I'd been dawdling because I'd been enjoying nature's spring spectacular. The hawthorn hedgerows bordering the lanes are wearing their white blossomy coats and look like breaking waves either side of the road. And I could hear the bees and smell the scent - delightful.

I'm sure it's the same with many people, in that much of the stuff that winds me up these days is not my fault - the stuff that niggles, like potholes in the road or spiralling taxes or lousy TV. It's all foisted on us by people over whom I have no control. But I have the antidote. I can handle the hassle because I am able to escape by pottering along on my bike. A comfortable environment typified by modest speed, pleasant smells and nobody to pull my chain. Until the mood is ruined by a sandwich-munching, interfering swine who pokes his nose in trying to be funny. He's probably a very nice man. And who knows what problems he may have. Perhaps his crop of leeks has failed and he's in desperate need of solace. He's probably using humour as a defensive tool. So I keep calm and don't respond to his jibe, unintentional though it may have been. I just accelerate away along the gravelly road, very much like a motorcycle racer leaving the grid at the start of a Grand Prix, leaving his sandwich covered in grit.

The Short End of the Stick

Notes from the Blue Planet by Frank the Terrier

Hi ho, ya all. Frank's back!

I've noticed that other 'authors' include quotes from fellow writers, so here's one that I feel adds a touch of gravitas:

Extract from the book, *To be a Dog* by Martin Creswell.

> *"Dogs have an approximate life span of between ten and eighteen years. Human beings have more like eighty. Considering each species' net value to Planet Earth, evolution seems to have gone slightly awry. Dogs have ended up, by some margin, with the short end of the stick. When one considers that dogs spend half their life in pursuit of a stick, 'the short end of one' is not only a regrettable turn of phrase, it's also an unfortunate statistic.*
>
> *The Upright species (in recognizable form) started*

about 200,000 years ago. Known incongruously as Homo Sapiens, today's 'wise men' look unlikely to last much longer. Why? Well, the way they are developing they'll soon have the capability of destroying the entire planet along with everything that lives on it.

Dogs on the other hand arrived only thirty-thousand years ago. They are much earlier in their evolutionary development and show tantalizing signs of evolving into the dominant species. They are becoming more refined with each generation. They are also developing ever-better specialist traits. For example, they are better sniffer-outers of things illicit. They are faster and better-looking and are much less likely to blow each another up. They often smell better, are generally fitter and don't drink as much.

Uprights on the other hand are going backwards while getting larger and larger. There's a reverse evolution thing going on. Start smart, end up messed up."

McTavish (Scottie and prodigious message-leaver) left a piddled memo on a goal post the other morning that caused quite a debate. *"What's going on?"* It said, *"The Uprights have developed a sudden insecurity about what to call themselves: man, woman, he, it, them ... what the hell's going on?'*

'Dogs have had similar problems for ages,' said Mad Lynne the Afghan (aka Madalene). 'Chop this, remove that and suddenly, from being distinctly one or the other, we're in a sort of no-dogs land.'

'We go to the dogtor as ferocious, red-blooded males,' said Bruce (lurcher), 'and come out half an hour later minus a couple of appendages, swinging a handbag instead of testicles.'

'Frank always did swing a mean handbag,' muttered McTavish.

'Shut it, you,' I said. 'Anyhow, my Dad had a good take on it. He said, with an unusual dose of common sense, *'Believe it or not, I was once a man trapped in a woman's body. Then I was born.'* Unfortunately, it upset plenty of people. The liberals because he seemed to be taking the piss, the humour police because it was gender-sensitive and Peter the bus driver because he spilled his coffee laughing.'

'Speaking of which,' said Doug, 'there goes Roberta who used to be Robert before he had his privates amended. Morning, Bertie,' he said, waving.

Roberta looked pained and headed off down the snicket, which is a euphemism if ever I heard one. (A snicket is an alleyway in northern England, otherwise known as a ginnel. In the south of England an alleyway is an alleyway - which is pretty unimaginative.)

'I think most Uprights who swap sides physically are just trying to attract attention,' said Bruce. 'They're deficient at anything worthwhile so go for the shock/awe approach so people will pay them attention.'

'Even if it's only to be told what a plonker they look,' muttered Mad Lynn.

'No, they love that. They love being insulted or marginalized. They can go on television and tell everyone how they've been persecuted. They moan about how they've been forced to have psychiatric therapy and, as a result of their woes, piled the weight on. Nothing to do with having an overactive set of kitchen cutlery, of course, which shovels rubbishy food into their porcine faces. No, it's seems that many of their difficulties stem from the fact that they've been sniggered at.'

'They blame it on water retention,' said Bruce.

'Blame what on water retention?' I asked.

'Getting fatter.'

'Food retention, you mean,' said McTavish.

'That's very insensitive,' moaned Doug, who is more rotund than than pointed. He continued dramatically, 'I think I'm going to have a meltdown and go into an expensive clinic for a month, paid for by a glossy 'victims' magazine.'

'You're a glossy victim then?' asked McTavish.

'The mag is glossy, you idiot, not me.'

'Ultimately, too many blame their woes on the pressure of being different,' said Bruce.

'And being a plonker,' said Mad Lyn.

'Misunderstood is a kinder way to phrase it,' muttered Bruce.

'Plonker.'

'Yes, you're probably right.'

There, as you can see from that brief passage, canines have basically resolved the pronoun problem. If only the Uprights could sort things out so speedily and effectively.

Later that evening , a group of Uprights gathered on the field. There had been talk of the authorities building a school on the football pitches, but the threat seems to have dissipated because whoever was to fund the scheme has run short of cash. The purpose of the meeting was to talk about how they could further encourage the council to drop the whole idea of a school, on these particular playing fields anyway.

'This is just typical of the Uprights,' said Julie (Spaniel). 'They come out and make a big fuss after the matter is over and done with. They're bucket-full of confidence now there's nothing to lose.'

'Aye, it's rather a toothless affair, isn't it? Basically, a lot of Willy waving,' said Willy the Whippet.

We dogs had gathered, some distance from The Uprights, in a group of our own, sniffing and piddling and chewing the fat, or anything else that has been discarded. Living life with gay abandon, if I'm allowed to say that. Many of the regulars were there. In addition to Willy and McTavish, there was Julie, Monica the husky, Shankly the Bichon Frise, Betty the Dalmatian and me, Frank. We were also joined by a new kid on the block. Technically he is a only a kid, being about eleven months old, but he's enormous. Delaney is an Irish Wolfhound, a gentle but imposing presence. His owner, Sean O'Brien, is himself a big, strapping individual who wears a threadbare cloth cap come rain or shine. (He's rather short in the follicle department if the truth be known, and he's too vain to have a comb-over on display).

Sean is a native of the Emerald Isle but moved to Littleborough about ten years ago, when his wife Mary told him to. She wanted to be near her sister Grace who, in Mary's words, 'is losing it.' Some pointedly suggest it was less concern for her sibling than the substantial four-bed detached that drew Mary over the Irish Sea. Whatever, Mary and Sean own and run the bakery on the high street, so they have blended in well. Annoyingly, Mary's sister is still lingering on. Indeed, she has rallied a bit recently, so Mary is being forced to wait for her inheritance – if Grace hasn't changed her will! Sean proudly boasts that Delaney is of good stock, a purebred of flawless 'paddygree' as he terms it. Nobody is quite sure if he pronounces it 'paddygree' because of his Irish accent, or as he really is clueless.

Sam wandered over. 'I've just put fish oil on my bicycle chain,' he announced with all sincerity. 'Speeded my bike up considerably – now I can show anybody a clean pair of eels.'

Cue smirks and titters.

'Don't laugh, Delaney, for goodness sake,' said Shankly. 'We'll never hear the end of it.'

'Listening to Sam shortens your life expectancy,' said Shankly.

'You can talk! All your gibberish about Liverpool Football Club, delivered via your usual mixture of barely intelligible non-sequiturs in the Scouse dialect.'

'That was a long sentence,' said Willy.

'Life sentence,' said Sam, 'being subject to Shankly's rambles.'

A fairly companionable silence descended. The Uprights could be heard muttering across the other side of the football pitch.

'Speaking of life sentence,' said Betty, 'have you noticed the Uprights always seem to be in a mad dash to reach the afterlife? They seem to come up with increasingly imaginative ways to make themselves more stressed.'

'I have to agree,' I replied. 'Look, even standing in a field talking about something that's not going to happen is getting them steamed up.'

'I think it's just that they like to talk. Or rather, they feel the need to say something important, something definitive. It's like they need to raise, or maintain, their standing. Not like us hounds who gently ramble through a discussion in a dignified manner.'

'Huh!' spluttered Sam. 'Shankly doesn't ramble, nor is he dignified. He charges through a conversation without the slightest regard for either his audience or the delicate nuances of the canine language.'

'Knickers,' said Shankly.

Bert rolled up, licking his lips. One of the best foragers is

Bert, but unfortunately he's got the reputation of being over-fond of other dog's dollops - with some justification it has to be said. Not on this occasion though; he looked to have a piece of hamburger bun stuck in his whiskers.

Bert approached me and said, 'I overheard my Upright talking to yours, Frank. It amazes me what they come out with. He said, quote, *"I think it's a disgrace on society and our education system when, after fifty years, most people have no idea who Neil Armstrong is. Or just how good he was at the trumpet."*'

Even I chuckled at that one. 'Doesn't surprise me in the slightest, Bert. Mine regularly comes out with gibberish. The other day he said that the air we breathe is poisonous. It just takes about seventy-five years to kill us.'

'Is that logical or dumb?'

'Thought-provoking.'

'Dumb.'

Chuckles all round.

'I only go and fetch the ball because I know my Upright likes throwing it,' said Hamilton, with his Bark and Ride trailer attached by a harness.

'Aye,' said Bert, 'that's a good way of looking at it.'

Walking down the cobbled road next to the park was Mr Clegg and his Golden Retriever, Bertha.

'Poor old Bertha,' said Doug. 'It's all very well being highly bred, but it doesn't half cause problems in the health department. She's at the dogtor at least once a fortnight for some ailment or other. Found out last time she's allergic to something in her food so they've had to change her diet again, which in turn gave her the trots.'

'Best off being like Frank,' said Monica. 'A mixture of hardy breeds. Generally impervious to malady even if he has ended up with a gait like an geriatric donkey.'

'Oi, I heard that,' I yelled at her. She only gets away with it because Monica and I are friends. And she's much bigger than me.

One thing we hounds discussed was the Upright's habit of hill climbing. Dogs will climb a hill for a specific purpose, like if there's a snack at the top, but in the normal course of events we avoid them. If our snack is on the other side of the hill we walk round, stay on the level. Except Bert that is; he takes the fastest route, however hilly. He can't bear the thought of somebody getting to a treat before him, however foul-smelling. An Upright, however, will don boots and bright clothing and climb a hill on purpose, just for the sake of it. Then they climb down again. It seems to us that hill climbing is an analogy of their lives. They face hills in different areas. The financial hill, for example, so they can buy a car with wider wheels or buy a bigger box to live in. When they've spent up, they start another hill. What a roller-coaster.

Divots and Dopes

Board meeting, continuance - June 24, 2021 - Earth calendar

'OK,' said Aidrian, 'let's just finish up with that pandemic I mentioned yesterday. You recall?'

TC nodded and blew his cheeks out, looking like he was preparing himself for a barrage of nonsense. Dog Almighty opened an eye.

'It was nothing earth-ending,' continued Aidrian. 'Nastier than some they've had but nothing that warranted the reaction it got. A major downside to the Internet is the opportunity to put the Earth into global meltdown in about ten earth minutes. Thanks to the Web, the Upright response has gone far and above anything remotely sensible. The problem is that one individual can shoot something off into the ether totally unregulated. There's no specific target so it can land in the plasma-box of any number of other Uprights. It takes only a few others to get steamed up and send it to their friends. One becomes ten, ten becomes a hundred and so on. Before your breakfast toast pops up a million people, all over the planet, are banned from going for a haircut.' Aidrian sighed. 'Can you make sense of it? Because I can't.

The Creator shook his head. 'Sadly not.'

'The frightening thing is that the very first message may be erroneous! It could easily be nothing more than the product of some lunatic's imagination. In fact, the number 500,000 set the whole thing off and it transpires that it was plucked from the imagination of some doomsayer with a crystal ball. Compounding the felony, Uprights would rather soak up a wild theory than listen to anything remotely logical. Once these falsehoods are ingrained in the human grey matter, it appears there is no reversing the process. Just this morning,' said Aidrian, 'the apostles unearthed some extraordinary developments.'

'Goodness, now what?' said Dog.

'The hysteria galloped round the globe faster than one of those nasty little satellite things they sent into space.' Aidrian smiled to himself.

'What is it?' asked Dog.

'Satellites. Just for the record, they were going to call the very first one 'Spunk-it' before we managed get one of our emissaries to infiltrate their programme. Thankfully, we managed to persuade them to change the name to 'Sputnik.' We really didn't want something with a name like 'Spunk-it' hurtling around the universe. What impression would that give to an inter-stellar visitor?'

'Ultimately, with this pandemic, all the Uprights had to do was to get themselves healthy and look after the older specimens, especially those who were already knackered. Instead, they gathered together a group of the greediest, most unpleasant people they could find and told them to engineer an expensive solution. What did they come up with? A never-ending series of injections! A serum that barely worked. In fact, it appears to have caused more problems than it solved. Honestly, you couldn't make it up!

'On all the planets we're monitoring this is probably the most bizarre behaviour we've ever seen. Except Xion-32 of course, which blew itself up trying to invent a food processor. Remember that?'

'I do indeed,' said TC with a look of horror. 'What a shambles that was. Chicken liver all over the cosmos.'

'Mind you, it shows how technologically advanced the Xionites are. The earthlings can't even make a dent in their planet with their biggest bombs. Not yet, at least.'

'There's now't more peculiar than folk,' said Dog knowingly, coining a phrase that would become commonplace in the northern reaches of one particular island.

'Aye, you can say that again,' muttered TC.

'At least you can relax, Dog, knowing that you didn't have anything to do with creating the Uprights. The damage was done well before you arrived.'

'True,' said TC, 'but the poor fellow has had to manage the results of our meddling. That can't have been easy.'

Dog just smiled.

Aidrian sighed before continuing. 'Just this morning we've received extraordinary footage from Earth showing thousands and thousands of Uprights walking around in random patterns. Many were bleeding steadily from all the pricks they'd received.'

'Finally, as I know it's getting time for your next nap, I'd like to bring to your attention the incredible things that went on in one region, a very large one and supposedly civilized, as they tried to elect a new leader. If you put it on the stage nobody would believe it. On the one hand, in the nutty corner if you will, we had the present incumbent who won some sort of popular vote a while ago. He's an extraordinary specimen who is independently wealthy – of material things that is, as opposed to having cerebral wedge. He made regular, unintelligible proclamations from his Oval Orifice.' Aidrian smiled to himself. 'Yes, some wag changed the script there, which is witty and wholly appropriate.

'Though I remain non-judgmental, the odd gem floats up here and I get pleasure from the fact that we've at least created something vaguely imaginative. Anyhow, this lunatic also enjoys golf, as do I, but he takes it to the extreme. Can you believe he wears a divot on his head? Quite a fashion statement, I can tell you. It flaps about in the breeze like the opening and closing of a clam. His electoral opponent was a man nearly as old as you, TC. He appears to struggle to remain awake and sometimes it's possible to see the strings that his 'advisors' use to operate him. Frankly, the whole debacle is rather embarrassing for such a large, conspicuous region, especially as it considers itself superior to everywhere else. Anyhow, the old man won and Mr Divot retired to his golf enclave to lick his wounds. I suspect we haven't heard the last of that drama.'

'I could go on, but just as a final point we have studied the fuel the Uprights use to propel themselves around; in other words, the food they eat. We gave them a wonderful assortment of fresh vegetables, fruit and meat in many forms. Sadly, only a small proportion is eaten as intended. In other words, if they ate decent stuff we could tell what they are eating by the shape of a particular item and it's odour, rather like Eve's first apple - just not as sinister. However, increasingly they take these lovely raw ingredients, evolved over millions of years, mash them into a mush, then add all sorts of rubbish to it. The resulting mixture is then re-formed into a new shape and called something else. A hamburger, for example, usually contains beef, not ham. And 'burger' is derived from the word for a wealthy medieval citizen. The whole thing is enclosed in two halves of an artificial bread with grit on top and padded out with noxious pickles. The taste is screened by a mixture of sauces which are by-products of various industrial processes. The last thing a discerning medieval noble would be seen eating is a revolting mishmash like that. Or me, I might add!

'In fact, what they've done is create the archetypal vicious circle. They eat these nutritionally bereft concoctions, then have to supplement their intake with tonne upon tonne of various extra vitamins and potions. Then, surprise surprise, they get sick and have to take medicines and balms manufactured for eye-watering profits by enormous chemical companies. It's just like a huge, revolting whirlpool spinning slowly in the cosmos. It's hardly surprising that so many arrive at our front gate looking like they're about to explode.

'Anyhow, that's it for now, TC. To sum up, if nothing else the experiment is fascinating. We have more to bring you, but I think that's enough for the moment. There are some wonderful nuggets on earth which, if nothing else, will make a good basis for future civilizations. But we'll need to be choosy. I think it's fair to say that when things were left in peace to evolve Earth produced some wondrous specimens. As I say, the problem came when the Uprights arrived on the scene. A bit too clever for their own good, perhaps? Or worse, they think they are. They're making a right god's breakfast of it. We've concluded that there may be less than an earth's century left for the experiment at its present rate of self-destruction. It's alarming, but there it is.

'Jesus Christ,' said The Creator. 'Mary's going to be furious. She's just bought a ruck of shares in GlaxoSmithKline.'

'Quite,' replied Aidrian.

© Marcus Cicero June 2021

Whirlpool of Benevolence

Another Note from the Blue Planet by Jo May

Recreation is a gift from the heavens. And boy, do we need to chill. We, that's Uprights male and female the world over, have created any number of ways to stress ourselves out. Money, daft regulations, taxes, relationships, weight worries, self-induced ill-health, idiots on television, dogs vomiting in the car, 'press one for this, press 2 for that ...' - the list goes on and on. What we haven't mastered are the antidotes. We haven't discovered the yang to yin's angst. There's eating chocolate but that is only a short-term fix, as is the demon drink. Both of those lead to ill health and yet more anxiety, which leads to more chocolate.

What we are particularly good at is ignoring the healthy option. Rather than hopping on a bicycle to rev up the endorphins, a natural stress-reliever, we crack open a bottle of gin or shout at the dog.

If we'd only seek them out, there are multifarious ways to escape the traumas of everyday life. Walking the dog is a good one. In my case that is *usually* relaxing. On occasions, Frank does take on a mind of his own. I'm left whistling and yelling as he rustles about in the undergrowth seeking out discarded burgers. My patience and well-being are compromised till he comes trotting up with a grin on his face, tail wagging. *'Sorry, didn't hear you shouting and whistling for five whole minutes. I must have been in an auditory dead spot.'*

Then we do things that are supposed to be relaxing, but aren't. They used to be, but they aren't now. Going for a Sunday drive, for example. Let the old girl stretch her legs (if you've remembered to plug it in to charge it). All's fine and dandy until we actually leave the avenue. Somewhere within the first fifteen yards out on the highway, we get stuck behind some berk in a flat hat who infuriatingly drives just under the speed limit. When they finally turn off we get stuck behind a peloton of bicycles riding two or three abreast, then a tractor towing a mountain of muck.

To avoid self-induced road rage you pull into a garden centre to chill out. An hour later you've somehow spent forty-eight pounds on a small shrub. Well, a shrub plus extras: coffee and cake for two, a pair of clove-scented candles and a book on embroidery, none of which (excepting the shrub) would have been temptations a generation ago when garden centres exclusively sold things for the garden. There are too many temptations. The answer? Number one by some margin is don't get a trolley on your way in. A trolley is like a shelf - you fill it. There are few sorrier sights than a large trolley with one tiny shrub in it, so you pile in a few stocking-fillers. Usually stuff that if you'd only take a second to think about it you probably don't need. Never mind probably - definitely.

When you finally get home to relax for the first time since you left to go on your relaxing drive, you need a stiff gin and a long nap while (not) watching Bridge over the River Kwai (again), a film that is nearly as ancient as the old git in the Vauxhall Viva and flat hat. Aaaannnd ... relax.

Another fun outing is a visit to a table-top sale. Frank touched on this in his book, but we've had the opportunity to experience one first-hand - by taking part. A table cost us ten pounds. For that 'investment' in our future, we stand there feeling very self-conscious as people walk straight past and head for the concession stand where you can get a very respectable cup of coffee and a lump of home-made cake for a donation to the church roof fund. We're in the church hall and one of about ten stall-holders. *'Thank god you're here,'* said a local councillor. *'You've raised the tone of goods on offer by some margin.'* That was flattering for us but seemed slightly unfair on the regular stall-holders, invariably long-term churchgoers and folk diligently 'doing their best.' People who have obviously taken great care raiding their 'stuff to go to the tip' pile to stock their stalls - with items that nobody can possibly want.

It's a wonderful marketing system, actually. Only people who are dedicated supporters of their particular church are willing to pay money for most of the stuff on offer. For example, though brand new (a number of years ago), and still with the price label attached (occasionally in pre-decimal currency, which was 1971!) it's not everybody who needs a cheese grater or washing-up bowl. People proudly take their purchases home but have no intention of using them, of course. No, they put them to one side until the next table-top sale when the goods will once again be offered and bought by another church supporter. It's genius, actually - nobody ever needs to source any new stock; it's all recycled in a great whirlpool of benevolence with the church roof at its centre. After all, these godly buildings require a bottomless pit of money to maintain them.

It's not just via table-top sales that products of dubious provenance get scattered throughout the community. My wife partook of a raffle at a local ladies group. Everyone had to bring a prize so nobody went home empty-handed. My dear wife was overwhelmed to win a tube of heel cream! Who the hell brings a tube of heel cream as a raffle prize? She'd arrived full of hope and optimism, carrying her offering for the raffle - a delicious box of luxury chocolates. She left, a little less full of hope and optimism, wondering where she could covertly offload a tube of heel cream.

BUT, she left with a smile on her face because she was told an amusing little story by a fellow member.....

My boss texted me yesterday, "Send me, one of your funny jokes".
I replied, "I'm working at the moment, I will send you one later."
He replied, "That was fantastic. Send me another one."

It's a poor do when, burdened with your raffle prize, you have to seek relaxation after a visit to your ladies' group. The funfair is in town, so ... pick up the grandchildren and head off for a spin on the waltzer. Actually, waltzer is old hat, these days it'll be 'Armageddon' or 'Death Star.' Both are guaranteed to have the youngsters scared witless (which is the whole point) and dashing for the ice-cream van. After all, a sugar rush is just what's needed to perk them up a bit! Top of the list here is candy floss, pure, neat sugar with a bit of colouring. I wonder why they don't have vegetable concessions?

You have to attend fairs during hours of daylight because after dark the booze and vomit crowd stagger into town. Rather like watching football, if you don't get either picked or beaten-up it's not a proper outing.

There are wonderful days out - country house gardens, for

example, where after a poke around in the first flower bed it's 'Can we go home now, Nana?'

Hot 'n' Cold

B *oard meeting. July 17th, 2021 - Earth calendar*

'Remember I mentioned how easy it is for a determined few to influence the many? We knew this to be true as far as religion was concerned; we only have to look at how much influence Aidrian had in his *'Son of God'* guise a couple of thousand years ago.

'Well, now it seems they've started a campaign to try and change the weather. Of course, we built temperature fluctuations into their long-term plan to see how they would cope with change. In addition, of course, these climatic changes shuffle the balance of animal and insect species which makes it all a bit more interesting for us watching.'

Dog coughed pointedly.

'Apologies, Dog. Not all species are struggling to adapt. You and yours have the wit and resourcefulness to live with change – thrive even. As we're all aware, there's every possibility that your canine companions may supersede the Uprights.'

'Mmm,' said Dog thoughtfully, his mind whirring.

'Anyhow,' continued Aidrian, 'it turns out these activists, who are opportunists at the end of the day with little better to do with their time, have jumped on the latest minimal temperature increase to see if they can create a state of fear and panic. Bit similar to the pandemic panic.

'The problem is that there are a minority of earthlings, perhaps as few as three percent, intent on maintaining chaos. It's amazing how few people you need to influence everyone else. It appears that if they shout loud enough a section of the most gormless even glue themselves to roads as a protest. Quite what lying in a pothole is going to achieve is anybody's guess. They are being led by a root vegetable from an area called Scandinavia. She's an impressionable, peculiar-looking creature who's been persuaded to stand in front of crowds and shriek. What we can ascertain is that one mouthpiece yelling loudly enough can encourage others into following the message. Particularly if there are enough present who are A) gullible enough to believe anything or B) who refuse to listen to any sensible counterargument or C) feel they need to have a cause in life to make it worthwhile.

'It's been quite amusing, really. We chose a region containing some of the most moronic individuals and just for devilment turned up the temperature for a few days to see what reaction we might get. It's a collection of badly matched ethnic groups called, quite incomprehensively, the United Kingdom. You've never seen such a manic over-reaction in your life. Just about the whole place ground to a stop and they sat inside their huts watching endless televisual repeats. Every other piece of news was put on the back burner (to coin a phrase) as the propaganda machine they call the media went into meltdown and blamed the blip in the weather for all sorts of bizarre events. Even when somebody set fire to a house they blamed it on the weather.

'Of course, this was manna from heaven (literally) for the climate lunatics. They claimed that because an old man in

Bournemouth (called Arthur) was using his gas boiler to have a shower, the country was suddenly sweltering. It was termed by the climate zealots as 'Arthur's Indiscretion' - more evidence that the selfish old gits are wilfully destroying not only their own retirement funds but, more importantly, the entire planet.

'One theme that Madam Root Vegetable wails about repeatedly, with her face scrunched up like an badly ironed vest, is that people like Arthur have stolen her future. Frankly, me and the Apostles are slightly nonplussed about this allegation and do consider it to be somewhat of an over-reaction. There are patently lots of honest people who don't steal anything. In fact, it rather looks like this small minority of activists appear to be stealing Arthur's present. When we investigated, one of the scribes found the following:

> *"Not far to the south of where the Root Vegetable howls and wails there's a place called the Menen Gate. It's on the site of one of their fierce historical battles. Thousands upon thousands of people died fighting for control of a desolate patch of mud. The monument is the final resting place of nearly fifty-five thousand people who died in battle. Every year many thousands come to see the memorial. We found that, without exception, not a single visitor believes that those remembered in the memorial stole anything from anybody, ever. In fact, they appear quite resentful of the accusation.*
>
> *The spirits of those who died look down with sorrow. They wonder if the present generation understands the sacrifice they made. But wondering is all they have. Because they are no longer earthly, they cannot respond. They do understand that the vegetable believes she is*

fighting her own battle, but question if it's really the right one."

'You'll be well aware how well and speedily canines have developed into a diverse collection of specialist breeds. They did it with intelligence and patience. I have to say, TC, that our colleague, Dog Almighty here, played a big hand in that. As a result of the success of the canine breeds, we have started informal discussions about how to develop other species - apart from the dominant Uprights, that is. The reasons are twofold. Firstly, it would increase the intensity of our experiment. It could answer how other species would react if we nudged one towards supremacy. Would others consider it a threat and react?

'Secondly, we may have to prepare the ground for the demise of the Uprights. They are proving mighty unreliable in some areas, health management and weaponry to name two. There are enough lunatics at liberty to cause a huge amount of damage should certain technological developments get into the wrong hands.

'Regarding allowing deities in different species,' said Dog, 'one of the things that turned us against the idea was when we considered a God of poultry, we felt that having a Chicken Supreme was a frankly ridiculous notion.'

'Quite,' chuckled Aidrian. 'At the end of the day, the consensus was that we should leave well alone and let evolution take it's place. I trust that you find that satisfactory, TC? At least for the moment.'

'Most satisfactory.'

'Anyhow, TC, that's it for now. I hope our report has been useful.'

'Thank you, it was most informative. I'll suggest that Mother

Mary offloads her pharmaceutical shares. After all, they are perhaps a touch controversial for us higher-ups to be associated with. Maybe she can re-invest in something like dog-training academies?'

'There's a taxi service that would benefit from an investment,' said Dog. 'I understand Hamilton is looking to expand his Bark and Ride business. There are many dogs requiring transport to and from training centres and places where they have parts of their anatomies amended. He's looking to recruit and train some new operatives. There's an opportunity for your good lady.'

'Thank you, Dog. I'll put it to her.'

'There's always the movie business. There's a whisper I've heard that a major new canine project is looking for funding. It's a remake of an old classic featuring Brad Pittbull and Kay Nine called 'The Dogfather.''

'Good one, Dog,' said Aidrian smiling fondly at his friend and fellow board member.

'Dogfather,' chuckled TC. 'Whatever next? OK, let's leave it there for now. Thank you both for your valuable input. Rather a curate's egg of a report, but hopefully there are enough positive indications to keep our experiment going for a while at least.'

'Right,' said Aidrian. 'I'm off to see if I can get this three-iron to behave. I'll see you both later. It's most frustrating. I might be able to walk on water without a problem, but hit a three iron straight? No chance.'

'Good luck with that,' laughed Dog. 'See you in due course.'

© Marcus Cicero July 2022

Complications

(Yet) Another Note from the Blue Planet by Jo May

Animals and Uprights both make homes. Or dens. While one group just gets on with it, the other turns everything into a right old drama. Dogs have a sniff then circle a few times before curling up in a ball and that's it, set for a seven-hour sleep. Uprights, often without the necessary skills, use an assortment of lethal equipment to try and create a 'bespoke' boudoir. They make lots of noise and a worse mess, all to the soundtrack of some fruity language. All too often they chuck the whole lot in a skip. Then they visit Ikea to buy something actually fit for purpose called Skög (or similar).

Of course, there are craftspeople suitably trained for particular jobs, those who have learned through training and experience. In fact it's a joy watching a skilled cabinet-maker at work. In the vast majority of circumstances, amateurs discover things are not as easy as they look. In fact, only so many cock-ups can be made before they run out of funds.

Here, in his own words, is a brief account of one Upright's experience ...

"By way of example, there is a knack to hanging a door and a lot can go wrong. To start with there's every chance you've misaligned the door casing so you're going to have to trim the new door to size. This involves saws, planes and sanders – and plenty of choice language and a mountain of debris. When the door fits, approximately, you've got hinges, handles, keepers and lock to sort out. More tools – chisels, hammer, set square and a drill. After you've hung and removed it a few times to make 'minor adjustments' you can finally sit back and marvel at your handiwork. 'Here, look at this, love. That's saved us a bob or two.' Then the carpet-fitters arrive and you have to remove the door yet again to hack some more off the bottom. In fact you have to hack so much off there's no wood left and you're into the honeycomb interior. You either leave it as it is, now pretty flimsy at the bottom, or fashion a piece of timber to insert into the bottom of the door. Many more wood shavings, more time, more ripe language. In the time you've taken to do hang the door your beloved has done a days work, been shopping, walked the dog and made supper. In the time you've taken over the job, a skilled joiner would have finished and been for a weekend break fishing in the Lake District.

'Is this supposed to happen?' asks my wife, who's walked into the garden holding a door handle.

She'd caught me at an awkward moment because I was sprawled on the grass after the collapse of a garden chair I had just repaired. 'They don't build things like they used to,' she offers in sympathy. 'I'd take it back if I were you.' The beechwood carver had probably been supporting various buttocks since the late 19th century but

I'd managed to transform it into a pile of driftwood in the twinkling of an eye – all because I'd decided to try out my new 'multi-tool' on it.

So as I lay on the lawn inelegantly trying to remove a splinter from my rear end my wife looks on in awe and admiration (and sympathy and embarrassment) while my neighbour hangs over his fence reconsidering his request to engage my services to repair his dog kennel. He's rather fond of his dog."

The point, illustrated in part by that account, is that Uprights overcomplicate things. Here's an example: they have a perfectly good mode of transport attached to the bottom of their legs. But for some reason they feel the needed to 'develop' – so invented the wheel. That wasn't enough so they invented a bike, then a car, then a train, then a plane, then a rocket. Then, as other Uprights invented alternative sources of power, they 'progressed' to an electric bike then an electric car ... see where this is going? Next it'll be a bamboo bike, then ... Lordy, Lordy. Then the bamboo runs out so it's no more bikes and cars. Not only will Giant Pandas become extinct, it'll be back to walking, exactly where they were in the first place. Back to their true deportment – upright!

To make things even more complicated, and to keep a growing population in employment, there are peripheries to consider with every phase of 'development.' From raw materials, through all the stages of design and manufacture to distribution. Then there's insurance and marketing. Every step of the way it's hugely intensive, both in materials and personnel.

Things used to be so simple. First, sit on a rock and decide you're hungry. Next, sharpen a stick. Then, go hunting and sit down to a family meal. Back in early history, Uprights ate what was available. It must have been invigorating in a way not knowing what's for tea. Alarming, perhaps, if there wasn't anything for tea. It depended on which beast wandered into range, and if they did. It could have been fox or ox, lynx or minks. Actually, about 300,000 years ago it would more likely have been woolly rhino or mammoth. Whatever, after a dessert of berries and nuts it was all over and done with in a couple of hours – the whole tribe satisfied after a hearty meal. Replete, they were ready for an evening's light entertainment. *(That's watching the moon and stars joust for position in the heavens as opposed to flobbing around watching Coronation Street.)*

Now, let's make a comparison. Just witness modern Upright's shambolic progression from sitting on a rock to postprandial contentment.

First, a rock is no good because the lady next door has a leather recliner. Yes, a bit of product envy, so an immediate upgrade is required, something that befits the princes and princesses reclining in their own castle. I wonder if ancient Upright played 'keep up with the Joneses' like modern Uprights? Maybe the really self-important Palaeolithic hunter had a rockliner to sit on! The problem is, at every stage of the journey, whether its chairs or food, there is not only inter-tribe competition but also a huge number of choices, which are almost limitless.

Take food. This ranges from *'fresh-from-the-sod'* meat and two veg, right through to a horrid collection of concoctions squeezed out of a processing factory's despatch gate (aka buttocks). All too often the 'fresh' alternative is overlooked in favour of convenience. In fact, just calling it the alternative is indicative of the point we're at on our culinary journey. In other words, imitation stuff has basically become the norm. Real food is not extinct but it's at about 11.58 on the evolutionary clock.

We can take a storyboard journey depicting the convoluted route from rock to repast. Modern Uprights don't even need to raise themselves off their posteriors to plan, order and consume a meal. It can all be coordinated, via DG's Internet, from mission control; in other words, the armchair in front of the TV. All you need is a flashing modem and mobile communications device - both, though certainly not cheap, are necessities of the modern age. Besides, the family next door has the latest model modem. In addition, that ever so nice out-of-work actor, the one you recognize but can't put a name to, is pushing them on TV. Yes, certain items of technology are a must. More than a must! When you're on eBay bidding against your neighbour for a leg of lamb, you simply have to have the speediest connection. This is not one-upmanship, this is life or death! A family could starve without the latest tackle.

In fact, with the food order the only time one needs to physically leave one's chair is to collect the stuff from the front door - everything else in the chain is done by somebody else. We've all become links in our complex modern world. Remember back in the old days there used to be a coal chute from the footpath direct to an internal storage area? There is a potentially lucrative business here, adapting that former system to in-house food delivery. It's a win-win. The delivery van pulls up outside, shoves the food parcel through a hole in the wall and, hey presto, it is delivered - via a chute - straight into a chiller cabinet next to your armchair. The food processing industry, distributors, shops, delivery personnel, even DG's Internet, do all the heavy lifting (and profit accordingly) while allowing the armchair incumbent to carry on with their virtual exercise routines (or have a nap).

In ancient times Palaeolithic man followed their prey across vast areas of tundra, through forests, across rivers, up hills, down dales, taking no more than they needed. This, of course, was before the advent of the chest freezer so unconsumed meat would have rotted, unless it was dragged up above the arctic circle and buried in an ice-hole. Problem was that you'd have to expend so much energy dragging a carcass all that way, you'd have to have another couple of hunts to sustain yourself en route.

These days the whole thing is reversed – we don't follow the herd, the herd follows us and we certainly don't cross any tundra. Every way we turn, everywhere we look, our food is displayed before us in glorious, processed technicolour. Television programmes are vehicles for the purveyors of instant (but tasty) grub. A thirty-minute programme lasts less than twenty because we're bombarded with e-numbers disguised as grinning children. Worse, every time we press a button or even *think* that something looks good, we become part of the universal food 'machine.' Suddenly, and magically, we're enmeshed into a matrix of algorithms that directs suitable food to our inboxes 'based on our purchase history.'

But these algorithm's do misunderstand at times. Many years ago I typed 'escort' into the search box while looking for a replacement car, and was rewarded with page after page of ladies wearing suggestive underwear. I was bombarded with lusciousness for weeks until I told my computer I was gay.

Misunderstandings can lead to wars, or battles anyway. Our language, though wonderful, should be handled sympathetically – by a poet, for example. But it can be confusing. Words with very different meanings can sound the same – homophones, they're called. Take Hawes and whores, for example. The former popped into my head while writing – likely because we are currently close to the wonderful Yorkshire village of Hawes, cheese mecca. Wensleydale, the current incarnation of the business, is custodian to a cheese-making tradition in the vale dating back to the year 1150.

The latter goes back even further and can (so I'm led to understand) be equally rewarding, but probably best not to use the credit card! Plus, had whores been prominent in the Hawes area we'd have had to draw a veil over the vale! Confusing, isn't it?

I can't work it out but I can muse (like my cat!). I throw thoughts and ideas up in the air and see what happens. Here's a muse! Because life in general is so confusing we seek refuge in our own groups, in the safety of our own bubbles. People are increasingly sensitive these days and we need to watch what we're saying so as not to cause offence. It used to be that we could smile a greeting at anybody. If you tried that these days you're likely to get a punch on the snout.

Perhaps we get what we deserve. By complicating things we've made a dungeon for ourselves where true freedom of expression is not welcome, at least by enough people to cause a stink. Perhaps it's not a coincidence that some of the most beautiful creatures live in some of the loveliest places. Locations appear to dictate what thrives where. Wonderful fish on the world's reefs, for example. Wonder heaped on wonder. And though there are fine fish in streams and rivers, neither the location nor inhabitants quite measure up. There are exceptions – the electric blue king of fishers is a king anywhere.

The highest concentrations of people are often found in the least salubrious places. Location and inhabitant appear to have dragged each other down. Having said that, the most beautiful creatures live cheek by jowl with other beautiful creatures and they eat each other, so there's a brutal streak even in paradise.

Good Things

S*upplementary Board meeting. January 17th, 2023 – earth calendar*

<u>Addendum.</u>

Aidrian and Dog Almighty are once more in the company of The Creator.

'Dog and I have been musing,' said Aidrian. 'We think our editing has been rather too severe. In other words, we chopped some positives out of the earthly reports, leaving you with an impression that's perhaps a little too downbeat. We saw your dispirited expression at the conclusion of out last meeting and, though we don't actually fear for your sanity, we thought it would be nice to finish on a positive note.'

'I thought I'd concealed my feelings; it appears not. However, I have to concur it was rather difficult to accept that a significant portion of what we created seems to be quite so, er, structurally fragile.'

'There's no need to be despondent, TC. One thing that is for sure – if the reports had contained endless accounts of fluffy success stories, you'd soon have lost interest. It's like when the Uprights take a vacation. Not that we really get involved with that sort of thing, but they, and those on other worlds, seem to need what they call 'a break.' It's not the easiest concept to grasp, actually, nor is their behaviour particularly logical. You see, they often go to places where they are unable to communicate due to language difficulties. Plus, these places often have a brutal climate so they sit in the full glare of the sun in their underwear till they part company with a layer of skin. Maybe there's a snake-like group-fest going on or it's part of some ancient mating ritual. I suspect we'll never fully know. In addition, they eat things of dubious provenance, quite outside their normal intake, that results in them spending hours on a lavatory. Quite how they enjoy these escapades is a mystery.

'However, when they return to their own homes, it's the stories about what went awry that they relate to the friends and relatives who had the good sense to stay at home. Nobody seems to want to hear about the nice things. People would rather learn that their holidaying pals had come off a motor bike or fallen over a cliff. It seems that disasters are an endless source of entertainment and give people something to laugh about.

'At the end of the day, the Uprights do have many redeeming qualities. Being able to laugh at their own misfortunes is certainly one, even when hobbling around with a leg in plaster after the latest disaster.

'Dog and I have discussed the Upright's behaviour at length and we conclude that the principal thing in their favour is their capacity for love and friendship. There is a small element who will kick someone when they're down, but the overwhelming majority demonstrate empathy and affection for their fellow beings, particularly if they are in trouble. Take illness; some go to extraordinary lengths to help others, often in unpleasant circumstances. They go out of their way to be caring and compassionate. It's a wonderful trait.

'Dog,' said Aidrian, 'you are in a good position to talk about the charitable aspect of the Uprights. You have first-hand experience, I believe.'

'Indeed. Our very own Frank is an example here. Through no fault of their own, many canines find themselves wandering the streets hungry and frightened. The Uprights have compassion for us and will take us in, give us shelter before finding us a new, safe home. Ironically, it's a small proportion of Uprights who cause the problems in the first place. There is a minority element who mistreat us. Thankfully, the good outweighs the bad many fold. The point is that, largely, canines are dependent on Uprights for food and comfort. Of course, we can manage on our own, but life on the streets can be harsh, particularly in the northern wilds of Littleborough where the weather really is most unpredictable – to be polite. This is why, ultimately, we put up with being yelled at and told to sit or lie down in daft circumstances. It's anything for a quiet life, really. In return, we give them friendship and make sure they get some exercise even when it's chucking it down.'

'Another thing very much in their favour is creativity,' continues Aidrian. 'Through writing, poetry and painting, for example, they create make-believe dream-worlds that, in part at least, make up for the shambles of the place they actually live in. They seem to need a positive distraction and there are plenty of Uprights who work their magic. The only shame is that their everyday world is one where they have created self-imposed challenges. Most of it just isn't real. Like their plasma boxes on which they watch endless hours of drivel while digesting food of dubious provenance, often items where a perfectly good natural skin has been replaced by a cardboard box.

'In between the bouts of televisual drivel they have things called adverts - or messages. It's here, while sitting in a zombie-like trance, thus open to suggestive ideas, they are shown pictures of shiny things they can't afford. But they decide they want them anyway and, as a result, focus all their efforts on reaping in more lucre so they can acquire more and more of the expensive material things that make up a fake world. The wonderful things they create and the beautiful stuff that has evolved, like flowers and all things natural, are relegated to second fiddle behind stuff that makes them feel more important than the next Upright. It's all a bit back to front.

'They created games. Let's take rounders as an example, a game where families play together on the beach. Nobody is quite sure of the origin of the name; perhaps its that they originally played with a lump of drift wood and a pair of rolled-up socks to imitate a ball. Or it's so called because they ran round in circles, or that those who played were predominantly round. Whichever, it was a relaxed, fun thing to do while shedding another layer of burnt skin.

'Now rounders as a game has a pleasant, relaxing tone to it. Then the game became a sport - the driftwood was replaced by a shapely wooden stick and the socks by a lethal leather projectile. The equipment upgrade and name change prompted a change of emphasis to something slightly more serious. Then it developed further and became professional where people are paid to throw said projectile at someone else, whose only defence is that thin wooden stick. At this point, for those participating at least, most of the enjoyment appears to goes out of it. Suddenly it has become serious and a business. They dress in funny clothes and can't speak because they have a mouthful of everlasting gum. The game has completely transformed from an event where families can have blazing arguments on the beach to an activity all about self-preservation, money and Range Rovers.

'The one thing that sport does do is allow those who are less cerebrally endowed to prosper in the material world. It's a good thing, really, because with the lack of coherent thought that some of them demonstrate you certainly wouldn't want them performing open heart surgery on you.

'Ultimately, there are many wonderful things. Throughout the globe the Uprights have created a wonderful set of languages with which they can inspire or slay, teach or slight. Quite why they made so many different ones is a bit of a mystery, but there you go. One saying that is pretty universal in any language is, *'The best things in life are free,'* to which Frank, in his inimitable way, added, *'Yeah, free of conditions.'* Yes, even free things can come with condition and be a curse.

'TC,' said Aidrian. 'I want to conclude with what Dog and I believe to be an incontrovertible truth and, you'll be pleased to hear, a positive ending. The island nation home to the town of Littleborough is unsurpassed when it comes to pageantry, pomp and ceremony. Whether it's weddings, funerals or anniversaries, they don't half put on a spectacular show. Gold carriages, military and ceremonial uniforms, marching bands and hoards of people watching. How on earth they get everybody singing from the same hymn sheet is beyond us, considering that in the normal course of events they can't even take a dog for a walk without having a shouting match with it.

'Other countries try and match the splendour but never quite get there. Some have developed their own marching styles that look to have come from the ministry of silly walks. Legs and arms end up in the most unnatural configurations. It looks most uncomfortable. Some of them augment the parades with displays of military might. Probably trying to divert attention away from the daft walks. So that's it, TC. We're just about up to date with things.'

'It's been enlightening. Thank you, both. Next time we meet I hope you've got your three iron working properly. We don't want any more equine casualties.'

'Don't remind me.' Aidrian shivered and blew out his cheeks.

'Just one final thing,' said Dog. 'There's a press release in from some archaeological society that's worth a read. I'll send a copy over for you.'

'Good, thank you. I look forward to that. I'll see you both soon.'

The Best Laid Plans

The LankyArchaeology Society (L.A.S.) was formed in 3008.

LankyArchaeology Society
PRESS RELEASE

For immediate release
September 14, 3022

During recent excavations a set of ancient plans was discovered detailing a series of cubes in Rochdale that have subsequently collapsed. The plans offer a clue as to the building strategy of people of the previous millennium.

The mysterious cubes appear to have been built as a temporary home to the metropolitan elite who governed the Rochdale area over a thousand years ago. The cubes were also home to Rochdale Library. But it was not always thus. A building was unearthed nearby (with the unlikely name of Touchstones) which previously housed the town's library. It was built of sterner stuff, called stone. Stone is a natural product as opposed to the inferior human-made materials from which the cubes were fashioned. These being largely panes of molten sand held together by a matrix of steel bars that appear to have originated in somewhere called The Orient.

Also discovered in the collapsed sandcastle were plans that indicate the repurposing of pleasant swathes of green territory into communal living areas where tightly-grouped, unattractive boxes, were built to house Uprights with an aversion to the countryside.

We at the LankyArcheology Society (LAS) are trying to fathom out the transport system to and from these new high-density-box areas. It appears that movement would have been impossible except by vertical-take-off vehicles. Up here in the Romancashire (the north) there was a VTOL machine called an 'arrier so perhaps that was their answer. From previous excavations it's clear that earlier forms of transport were not up to the task. One simply ran out of steam and another became gridlocked as millions of 'wheely-boxes' were thrown at the transport problem, to the point where the highways were locked solid. We discovered endless lines of rust where vehicles, unable to move, were simply abandoned like long, rotting ribbons.

The strategic development plans were in two stages. Firstly, playing fields were laid down so young uprights could play football. This was an activity where little people, chasing an inflated sheep's bladder, ran about while being shouted at by bigger people. The game ended when a whistle was blown by a serious-looking being dressed in black. This appeared to trigger widespread relief. The little people returned to the safety of their virtual worlds, housed on a variety of gadgets, where they were either trampled by dragons or mauled by sabre-toothed

Wookies. The big people went home for breakfast, which consisted of slices of pig and solid dollops from a chicken's rear end. It became apparent that the sportspeople were only temporary custodians of these green and pleasant plots. They were merely treading water until …

Stage two. Plans revealed an intense box-building programme making 'efficient municipal use' of the unproductive green fields. This inevitably followed a lengthy period of negotiation where envelopes, usually brown in colour, were passed from workmen in boots to officials in suits. The latter often required medical intervention due to an ailment common to the period called 'backsackitis.' This presents as an uncomfortable swelling of the rear pocket.

These nasty contusions were inevitably followed by the appearance of swathes of unimaginative boxes. The phrase 'Pushing the Envelope' originally meant *'innovation or skill employed to create something that may surpass normal limits.'* However the phrase was repurposed in relation to box-building. Here it meant sliding an envelope surreptitiously across a table.

A stone tablet, also discovered in the wreckage of the cubes, offered a tantalizing clue as to the results of certain metropolitan elites' endeavours. The tablet was inscribed with the Romancashire phrase:

Inanimalia pixides pretium per tergum sacci

Which translates as:

Soulless boxes paid for through the back sack

The new dwellings lasted barely a century before they crumbled into rubble. However, they didn't go to waste. The thrifty people of the day used the resultant debris for the bed of a super-highway between Heaven and Hell, aka Lancashire and Yorkshire.

Ends:-

Jo

(A brief supplement written by Jo. Rather personal, even self-indulgent, but noteworthy.)

My imagination is both a wonder and a curse. It's all on the day. Sometimes I'm full of hope, at other times reflective - the latter usually happens when it's chucking it down or my shares have dropped!

With the advancing of the years there's a double whammy. We move slower but time speeds up. Before we know it, the rear-view mirror is filled with an ever more confusing infusion of sweet memories and missed opportunities. Although we remember much of what's gone, we are unable to recapture our experiences to either embrace them once again or to right wrongs. Some days I love the sounds and the smells and embrace the wonderful life we lead - the future appears to stretch on infinitely. On other occasions, time races by and the only apparent way to slow it down is to do the washing-up, a task that seems to take forever. There's always one more pan.

The dog cheers me up by his sniffing and snooping, happy thing that he is. The other day, though, I was nearly overwhelmed by melancholy when walking with dear old Frank. Though still pretty sprightly, he is getting on in years. There will come a time when he's called home. All of a sudden my heart ached at the thought of being without him. We've shared precious times at the break of dawn and together we have drawn the first breaths of many new days. He's listened to my frustrations and I've even tried out my jokes on him. He's been my good friend and confidante.

But, suddenly, I imagined him not being here. I experienced a flood of adrenaline and a rising of panic. Even now, seeing him squeeze through a gap in the hedge, reappearing after a forage, I can't dispel my angst. I'll miss him terribly, I know I will.

Frank

The sun is peeking over the hilltop. Contrails, stark white, streak across the crystal clear sky. No wind, no sound I know he's up there in the embrace of the deep blue. I just can't see him or hear him. Poor Dad. It was so sudden. Boy, do I miss him.

The Creator

N*ot long into the future.*

The Creator is sitting on his ornamental throne, the one he uses for audiences with invitees. On his left is Aidrian, on his right is Dog Almighty. Opposite, a few feet away, sits Jo - on a fishing stool.

'Sorry about the chair,' says Aidrian. 'The usual one is away for repair after a porker sat on it and broke it.'

'It's no problem. I'm honoured to be here,' he replies (although he did wonder how such an exalted set-up couldn't run to a spare chair).

'Thank you. You are indeed most welcome,' says Dog Almighty.

'May I say,' adds The Creator, 'how much we enjoyed the correspondence from your time on earth. Most enlightening, if sobering at times.'

'Glad you enjoyed it. There is plenty to write about, not all of it positive. Some things, stupidity for example, are very difficult to gloss over.'

'Indeed. We have noticed a number of vagaries and inconsistencies regarding the Uprights.'

Set into the floor between the deities and Jo is a portal through which can be seen the whole universe.

'Put those 3D goggles on,' says Aidrian. 'They're on the table next to you. It brings things to life.'

Jo dons them and is rewarded with an explosion of colour and depth. Galaxies, individual suns and vast, brightly-coloured nebulae fill his vision.

'Wow, that's amazing', he enthuses. 'Can we see Earth?'

'Sadly not these days. It is too small,' says The Creator, 'and it's tucked away in one of the most distant galaxies. The Milky Way, as they've called it, is moving away from us at close to the speed of light and we're still working on a camera that can keep up.'

'It's only taken four billion years,' mutters Aidrian.

'Patience, my friend,' says The Creator. 'There's no great hurry. Besides, at some point it'll slow down and eventually everything will start to come together again. The circle of life will one day be complete.'

'Recently we've been relying on your reports and those of Frank the dog,' adds Dog, 'but I suppose we'll catch up in real time eventually.'

They are all quiet for a moment as they watch the magic through the portal.

Then Jo says quietly, 'Talking about Frank, I never got chance to say goodbye. Is there anything I can do?'

'Sadly, no,' says The Creator. 'There are only a few specialized 'intermediaries' who can communicate between here and Earth, that's how we received your reports, unfortunately Frank is not one of the chosen few. We decided early on that all creatures must learn to make the most of their brief time in the earthly realm. Uprights, in particular, have to learn to communicate and not leave things unsaid.'

'I feel sad for him.'

'Don't fret, you'll meet again soon enough.'

The Creator points to his right. 'Through those doors is a parallel consciousness. It's where all souls go when the mortal cycle ends. You'll be pleasantly surprised, I'm sure.'

The End

(for now)

About the Author

I live in Littleborough with my wife Janna and dog, Tache.

Jan and I have both lived here on and off for over 60 years.

I began writing monthly articles for a canal magazine in 2007. Catastrophically (for the magazine), following an editorial misunderstanding, we parted company. Yes, I was sacked. I began to chronicle our travels which ultimately resulted in my three 'At Large' books, beginning with *'A Narrowboat at Large.'* I describe the books as a huge collection of warm memories, a library on which Jan and I can draw during long winter evenings and which will help us through our rocking-chair years. Magical times.

After destroying the UK's canal infrastructure on two narrowboats and rearranging a fair amount of continental waterways heritage on a rusty old Dutch Barge, our boating days came to an end in 2015, to everyone's relief except ours.

Boating days behind me, my new challenge is an e-bike. However, to mix metaphors, it's not all been plain sailing. *A Bike at Large* is written in homage to all portly, sub-standard cyclists, of which I am one. *Ordeals on Wheels* sums it up quite nicely.

I've also written three novels in addition to three 'little' books, namely The Boro, Let's be Frank and this one.

You can connect with me on:

🌐 https://jomay.uk

📘 https://www.facebook.com/JoMayWriter/?ref=bookmarks

Also by Jo May

Gods, Mortals and Mutts is my third mini book.
 It includes **The Creator's** eye view of where the word is today.
 He made it, but what's happened since!
 (It's possibly too daft to be a text on an exam syllabus!)

My first two mini books are **The Boro and Let's be Frank**. See below.
 This book completes the 3-book series: **Gods, Mortals and Mutts.**

My 'At Large' series comprises three boating books and a cycling one:
 A Narrowboat at Large (below)
 A Barge at Large
 A Barge at Large II
 A Bike at Large

Three novels:
 Operation Vegetable
 Twice Removed
 Flawed Liaisons

They are all here on my website: jomay.uk

The Boro

Returning to Littleborough after a break of nearly thirty years, I hope nothing's changed. But, inevitably, it has.

Like many folk in their seventh decade, I'm haunted by the spectre of how good things used to be.

It takes me a while, but I realize the past mustn't dominate; it must don a pair of slippers, settle into a comfy armchair and watch our future unfold. We have to create a new now in a place we're happy to live, both geographically and emotionally.

These impressions of a chap battling to blend with a modern world are also my light-hearted and daft take on a place I love, and dedicated to the memories of times gone by and for tomorrow.

Let's be Frank

.... a dog's eye view of the world.

Frank is a terrier / poodle cross - either a pooter or a troodle in the lexicon of designer dogs.

This little book is Frank's attempt to explain why human beings (Uprights as he calls them) have made such a hash of things.

Dogs have evolved in many disciplines, from ratting to rescue. They've become a collective of specialists, yet all share the same uncomplicated outlook on life.

He touches on topics such as education and religion but largely concentrates on things that really matter, like eating and friendship.

A Barge at Large

.... a dog's eye view of the world.

Frank is a terrier / poodle cross - either a pooter or a troodle in the lexicon of designer dogs.

This little book is Frank's attempt to explain why human beings (Uprights as he calls them) have made such a hash of things.

Dogs have evolved in many disciplines, from ratting to rescue. They've become a collective of specialists, yet all share the same uncomplicated outlook on life.

He touches on topics such as education and religion but largely concentrates on things that really matter, like eating and friendship.

A Barge at Large II
This volume continues Jo and Jan May's European adventure on their old Dutch Barge, Vrouwe Johanna.

Using skills learned as a baker in years gone by Jo transformed a neglected, scruffy boat into something fit to live on, at least for a couple with low expectations.

For two years they cut their teeth in Holland, remodelling their boat then learning to handle it on large lakes and quiet canals (where they couldn't do too much damage) before moving on to rearrange the infrastructure of the French waterways. According to their mate Dave, they finally reach the 'not totally incompetent level where other boaters at least had half a chance of returning to port undamaged'. They eventually run out of people to annoy in France and move on to Belgium where they find a new collection of victims.

Incorporating further boating tales, a short road trip and a shambolic introduction to camper vans this episode sees them expand their horizons and begin an uncoordinated search for a life after boating.

'I have always believed that you only get the chance to do something special for the first time once. Don't bother what is round the next bend, that will come soon enough, try and make the most of now because once you've turned the corner it's too late. All we have to look back on is today, so make it count.

Did we make the most of it? Very nearly.

Would we do it all again? No, it would never be the same.'

A Narrowboat at Large

is the first of three best-selling boating books in Jo's At Large series.

'So why did we take to the water? My wife can't swim, the dog hates it and I prefer beer. The main reason is that my wife's doctors had told her she was in real trouble so we developed a different perspective about the future than many people. We needed to get on with things.

We knew nothing about narrowboats and how we would cope being cooped up together – particularly when it's minus five and the nearest shop is miles away. We had a mountain to climb – which you can only do by using locks - and we'd never done a lock.

A more accurate analogy is shooting the rapids. Our venture took on a life of its own and we were washed down stream on a tide of enthusiasm and ignorance. We had to make it work or the people who had laughed and scoffed that we were mad would be proved right.

Well, make it work we did, and we boated for twelve years – first on narrowboats then an old barge on the continent.

It was marvellous and it possibly saved Jan's life.'

A Bike at Large

When he was overtaken by a jogger on a borrowed mountain bike, Jo knew it was time for drastic action. Welcome to the world of a man in his 60s and his new e-bike.

His first injury occurred within one foot! Setting off for his first practice ride round a car park, he misjudged the width of the handlebars and scraped his hand on the cycle shop's stone wall.

'You'll go places you'll never have dreamed of,' said the shop owner. Prophetic words indeed. Eighteen hours later Jo was embedded in his neighbours hedge due to a clothing malfunction. Fortunately, before setting out he'd put his ego and self-esteem in the top drawer in the kitchen.

With the emergency ambulance on speed-dial, Jo climbs a steep learning curve on a series of mini adventures throughout the north of England, mercifully with a diminishing distance to injury ratio.

By calling his e-bike a 'Lifestyle Investment', it took his wife's mind off the cost. At the time she needed some new slippers, so it was a sensitive issue. Asked whether he was searching for eternal youth? 'Not really,' he said, 'more trying to keep out of my eternal hole in the ground.'

Fuelled by red wine and optimism, off he goes………

Flawed Liaisons

Harry Dunn is an ordinary man living an ordinary life. But a series of events turn his world upside down. His life implodes and he is forced to run.

He is on the ragged edge when a surprise inheritance offers him a lifeline. But it's a poisoned chalice.

He hides away in the underbelly of a prosperous market town among the destitute where he befriends Mary, a woman tormented by her own demons.

Both are forced to confront their pasts as they try to unravel the mystery at the heart of Harry's downfall. What they discover is evil from the past that refuses to die – depravity carried through time in black hearts.

Harry and Mary forge a bond, a liaison born from the misery of their pasts. They have both suffered but find that others have paid a far higher price.

Operation Vegetable

Deep in the English countryside is Watergrove marina, home to a group of unlikely characters living on their narrowboats.

Life is carefree until a local land-owner decides he wants to build three luxury houses on the resident's vegetable plot.

Step forward Judy, a lady of physical substance, fierce determination and jocular disposition, who leads our ageing boaters in a counter-offensive code-named 'Operation Vegetable'.

H.Q. is the local pub and it's here that our ageing boaters raise a creaking battalion.

The boaters find help from an ageing rock star and a TV Gardening programme. Skirmish follows skirmish until one of the boaters is severely injured and the stakes are raised.

Has the despotic land-owner, a man of few morals, driven by power and greed, finally met his match?

Can the boaters overcome this scourge - or have they simply lost the plot?

Twice Removed

Welcome to the beautiful north of England where we encounter a wacky assortment of characters in a town called Thistledean, a curious place that nestles in the foothills of the fells of Northumberland.

It is a unique place, a blend of the recent past and distant past, held together by a community that feverishly protects its way life. They prefer the patina of aged leather and walnut veneer to the maelstrom of the modern world. They have been this way for generations. Residents are wary of anything that could upset their equilibrium but ultimately, Thistledean is a warm place.

Friendship is our most treasured possession and during our visit to Thistledean we discover the touching story of an ageing couple, strangers, who find a close friendship neither sought nor expected. They help each other in very different ways and their companionship develops into what Julia describes as a 'crinkly love affair'.

But there's a darker side to the tale where Julia gets herself into serious trouble while trying to unravel her past.

Printed in Great Britain
by Amazon